D0708346

DAD DISASTERS

'Never trust a man who when left alone with a tea cosy doesn't try it on.'

Billy Connolly

DAD DISASTERS

When Dads Go Bad

Ian Allen

PORTICO

CONTENTS

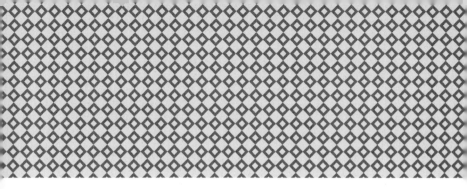

INTRODUCTION

Perhaps I should begin this introduction by warning people who have picked up *Dad Disasters* in the hope of reading some sort of sub-genre of the ever-popular misery memoir that they will be disappointed. Wait, though! Don't put it back! If your normal reading matter is the mis-mem, then in my experience you could certainly do with a good laugh. After all, there's nothing like a witty, well-crafted, humorous book to take your mind off things, and this is… a typical example of exactly the type of corny old Dad gag you'll find sprinkled between the stories in the following pages.

So, returning to our topic, which is where I think I was when I was interrupted by the wrong person picking up this book: the *Titanic*; the *Hindenburg*; the Tay Bridge collapse. These were all genuine, bona fide disasters, tragedies causing multiple loss of life and distress for thousands. They weren't funny when they happened, and if we can laugh at them now through the wrong end of the telescope of time (e.g. How do you think the unthinkable? With an itheberg), surely it's only because laughter is such a wonderful insulator against the pitfalls of life, both large and small. So the few real disasters that have worked their way into the book all come under the category of 'lessons from history' – not that Dads are very good at learning lessons.

A Dad Disaster, on the other hand, is a completely different kettle of fish. A Dad Disaster is funny from the moment it happens, for everyone except Dad. Within these pages you'll find dozens of dopey Dads making three things: ridiculous mistakes, daft errors of judgement and a fool of themselves, including the Dad whose attempts to discipline his son with tough love backfired when his son became more of a tough than ever; the Dad who in attempting to smuggle drugs into prison to his son made an ass of himself; the Dad who didn't notice his son climbing inside an arcade game; and the Dad who thought it was a good idea to go dancing with crocodiles.

I've also tossed in a selection of random, unverifiable, silly things that various Dads of family and friends have apparently done down the years, as passed on to me in confidence. I won't embarrass my friends, bearded or otherwise, further by identifying who did what, but the following people have either passed on recollections, or are the subject of them, so I'd like to say a big thank you to, or acknowledge a fond memory of: Frank Allen, Michelle Bullock, Shaun Bullock, Robert Barnard, Bill Brevitt and David Hall.

In addition, I've also tenuously lobbed in a few snippets of Dad trivia, lists and collections that I found interesting. If you don't, there's not much I can do, I'm afraid – after all, as the old saying goes, if you've enjoyed reading this book half as much as I've enjoyed writing it, then I've enjoyed writing it twice as much as you've enjoyed reading it.

Finally, no Dad book would be complete without a smattering of jokes, as we take time out now and again to imagine how things would turn out for your average Dad were he to set out on his dream career as a stand-up comic. To give you just a flavour of the standard of these, here's one that there wasn't room for.

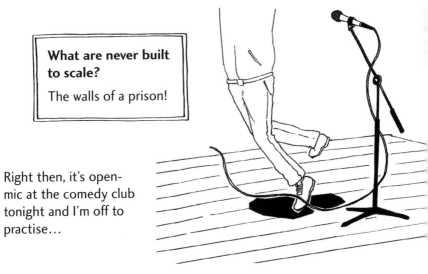

What are never built to scale?

The walls of a prison!

Right then, it's open-mic at the comedy club tonight and I'm off to practise…

TATTOO DISASTERS

Unshrekognisable

We all love our daughters, don't we, Dads? And we love showing off our snaps of our little princess. But about ten years ago one Dad took it a bit far when he decided to combine his love of his daughter and his fondness for tattoos by getting his leg emblazoned with a permanent likeness of his little Sophie.

So far, so good (if you like tattoos, that is). But the artist that our Dad, Malcolm, entrusted his left calf to turned out to be the William McGonagall of the tattoo world, and the result was far from a picture. Malcolm said it looked more like Queen Elizabeth than his daughter, a comparison that a few hundred years ago would have seen him sent to the Tower. His other daughter's description of it as an 'alien' is probably more accurate, though I personally reckon it's quite princess-like, as anyone who has ever seen *Shrek* will agree.

As you would hope, it all ended happily ever after for Malcolm and Sophie when Channel Five's *Tattoo Disasters* stepped in, and in 2015 the offending tattoo was skilfully altered by someone who knew what he was doing to a nice display of roses. Go online if you want to make your own mind up, where you'll find a proper picture of the lovely Sophie.

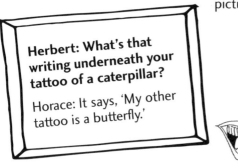

Herbert: What's that writing underneath your tattoo of a caterpillar?

Horace: It says, 'My other tattoo is a butterfly.'

Matt's Dreams in Tatt(oo)ers

In September 2015, the *Daily Mirror* reported how one Dad's ambitions to become a copper were put on hold when he was turned down by Kent Police.

Matthew Burns seemed like an ideal candidate for a special constable: good character, young, fit, a volunteer with the St John's Ambulance Brigade for ten years. So what was the problem? Was he too small to fit the helmet? Perhaps his voice wasn't low enough to pass the ''ello, 'ello, 'ello' test? Maybe he couldn't quite get sufficient sarcasm into his voice to deliver the line 'Well, well, well, if it isn't Stirling Moss/Nigel Mansell/Lewis Hamilton?' in a satisfactory manner.

No. Poor old Matthew was turned down because he had two 'potentially offensive' tattoos on his arms. One was of an alien, the other was a skeleton, which you'd have thought would be quite handy for a first-aider – 'Hold out your arm, Matt, I just want to check which bone he's broken…'

Anyone would think the long-sleeved shirt had never been invented. And what Dad hasn't done something in his past that's come back to bite him on the bum? Here's hoping that a bit of sense will prevail and Matt, covered or uncovered, will soon be pounding the beat.

Worst Tattoo Motto Mistakes

 Nobodies Perfect

 A Tattoo Is For Lif

❤️ No Regerts

❤️ What Does Not Kill Me Makes Me Stranger

❤️ Failure Is Not An Optoin

CRIMINAL DISASTERS

Byron Perkins and Destin, 'is Child

It's well known that having kids costs an arm and a leg, but rarely a kidney, and certainly not for a man the US media took delight in dubbing the 'world's worst father', Byron Perkins. In January 2006 Perkins, who had already served time for bank robbery, was awaiting sentencing after being convicted on firearms and drugs charges. Under uncompromising US law he was looking at a 25-year stretch.

You wouldn't expect him to be given bail in the circumstances, but he impressed the judge with the sincerity of his concern for his teenage son Destin, who was on dialysis and in vital need of a kidney transplant. Perkins was released in order to undergo tests to see if he could donate a spare organ to his lad.

So far, despite him having a criminal record, Byron sounds like a doting Dad, not a disastrous one. Alas, after initial tests proved inconclusive he was bailed again to attend more medical examinations. This time the temptation to leg it was too much and Perkins was last seen heading for the Mexican border, his backup kidney still very much inside his body.

Law enforcement officers expressed disgust at him for abandoning his son to his fate, and when he was finally tracked down and extradited he was banged up for 42 years. Destin, happily, reportedly received a kidney from another family member and is now doing well and is a Dad himself – and hopefully a more conscientious one than Byron.

Stuff My Dad Did

'My Dad once really said, "Good Consternoon, Afterble" to a policeman "for a laugh" when he was stopped for not having a working tail-light. The policeman enjoyed the joke so much he breathalysed him!'

Just Let It Go, Michael

I don't know how much of a disaster Michael May's Dad must have been, but in 2015 the Kentucky man was arrested for trying to dig up his father 30 years after he'd been buried to argue with him. It seems drink may have played its part...

Horace: Do you know any jokes about kidneys?

Herbert: I know one, but it's offal.

Herbert: Where have you been?

Horace: I've been burying my mother-in-law.

Herbert: Well, what are all those scratches?

Horace: Oh, she put up a hell of a fight.

Stuff My Dad Did

'My Dad ran out of wallpaper paste just before finishing the room, so used a combination of Pritt stick and Sellotape on the last bit "because it'll be behind the telly anyway". '

DIY DISASTERS

'Not Bad, Just Stupid...'

… is an epitaph that would surely satisfy all but the most optimistic of Dads, and it was the verdict passed down by a Leicester Crown Court judge to a certain Christopher Pendery in 2004. Mr Pendery, bless him, was only trying to make his home better for his children, giving them a nice room to play in by converting the loft. Like most Dads, however, he seriously overestimated his DIY skills, lining the floor of the loft with chipboard that wouldn't support any serious weight, and creating a more spacious, airy environment by sawing through roof-supporting timbers.

On top of all that – and explaining why he ended up in court – he didn't even own the house; it belonged to a housing association. After Christopher had finished with it, one surveyor described it as the 'most dangerous inhabited property' he'd seen in 11 years… experts, eh? What do they know?

Chris got away with 160 hours of community service… hopefully they didn't set him to work fixing pensioners' homes up.

Dad got fed up of doing it himself so put a card in the paper shop advertising for a handyman. When a chap turned up, Dad was keen to set him to work…

Dad: Could you install a new electric socket?

Handyman: No, I couldn't do that.

Dad: Well, could you put me some shelves up?

Handyman: No, I couldn't do that.

Dad: OK, could you at least paint my back yard?

Handyman: No, I couldn't do that.

Dad: Then in what way do you consider yourself a handyman?

Handyman: Well, I only live round the corner.

DIY Dad List

Eight things Dads love to send their kids to get from Mum.

1. A long weight (or a long stand)
2. A new bubble for the spirit level
3. A can of striped paint
4. A left-handed screwdriver
5. A jar of steam
6. Some elbow grease
7. A brick stretcher
8. Some holes for the nails to go in

TECHNOLOGY DISASTERS

Predictive Text Disasters

I never use predictive text myself, being a bit suspicious of it, but someone told me that they occasionally go wrong with – as they say in the tabloids – hilarious results. I had a bit of a peek online and I can tell you they're mostly far too rude for this book, so don't look them up whatever you do. Promise? Good. They obviously share this quality with limericks, about which it has rightly been said:

> The limerick packs laughs astronomical
> Into space that is quite economical,
> But the good ones we've seen
> So seldom are clean,
> And the clean ones so seldom are comical.

I did find one that I can repeat, from the letters pages of the *Daily Telegraph*, when a Mum sent her daughter a text while Dad was helping her with her homework (it sounds implausible, doesn't it). 'What do you want from life?' it said. The father and daughter pondered this unexpected existential question for a few minutes until the correction came through: 'Sorry, what do you want from Lidl?'

What was the spider doing on the laptop?

Looking at a website!

15

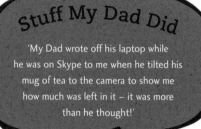

Stuff My Dad Did

'My Dad wrote off his laptop while he was on Skype to me when he tilted his mug of tea to the camera to show me how much was left in it – it was more than he thought!'

No Way!

Apparently the latest trick for tech-savvy kids is to get hold of Dad's mobile and change the predictive text settings so that when Dad tries to type 'No' instead it sends 'Yes', or 'Go ahead'. Then when Junior texts Dad to ask if he can have a party or stay out all night, he gets the answer he wants.

And of course your average Dad is extremely unlikely to be able to know how to change it back again.

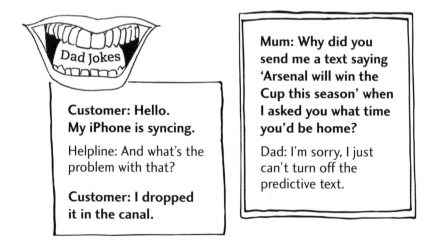

Dad Jokes

Customer: Hello. My iPhone is syncing.

Helpline: And what's the problem with that?

Customer: I dropped it in the canal.

Mum: Why did you send me a text saying 'Arsenal will win the Cup this season' when I asked you what time you'd be home?

Dad: I'm sorry, I just can't turn off the predictive text.

Dad Turns the Air Blue...
and the Room

And in 2015 an anonymous Dad hit the headlines online when a long sweary text conversation he had about his daughter's bedroom went viral. The odd thing was that his first text – 'Don't try and tell me I can't paint it blue because she's a girl!' – went to a wrong number, but the recipient was very understanding, and helpful, and went on to suggest picking out turquoise on a feature wall and making the others a little lighter for contrast. After all this free interior design advice, Dad seemed a lot calmer.

A Brief History of @!**! Time

Professor Stephen Hawking is now almost as famous for his appearances on *The Simpsons* as his ground-breaking research and best-selling books. But when his son Tim was younger he programmed his Dad's voice synthesizer with swear-words.

Dad Jokes

Horace: I see that Stephen Hawking has finally written another book.

Herbert: Yes, it's about time.

FORGETFUL DISASTERS

Is There Something I've Forgotten?

We all struggle to remember everything in the hurly-burly of modern life – keys, wallet, mobile phone, etc. And how much harder must it be if you're in a high-powered job with 24/7 demands on your attention?

So I'm sure we all sympathise with the daft Dad who left his local pub one Sunday lunchtime in 2012 after a convivial drink only to discover when he got home that he'd left behind… his daughter. Exhaustive research has identified this particular Dad as a Mr D. Cameron of Downing Street, London.

Yes, our beloved PM earns his entry in our book for accidentally abandoning eight-year-old Nancy at the Plough in Cadsden, Buckinghamshire, near Chequers. It was the classic case with which so many two-car families are familiar: 'I thought *your* security guards had our daughter'; 'No, you said *your* Special Branch officers were looking after her.'

Everything ended happily and Nancy was collected after 15 minutes without suffering permanent abandonment trauma. The Great British Public were sympathetic, as illustrated by some of the comments on the BBC News website:

'I am absolutely appalled!' said Sue, while Kay added: 'How anyone can possibly leave their own child behind in a pub is beyond me!'

Steve, meanwhile, used it as an opportunity to open another front in the class war: 'It is standard practice for the British rich to abandon their kids.'

But it was left to the appropriately named Daniel to throw a bit of biblical perspective on the whole business: 'Jesus at the age of 12 was left behind by his parents…'

No Publicity

Poor old DC, of course, had his Dad Disaster splashed over the front pages; the blushes of a Massachusetts Dad in May 2015 were sensitively protected by police who declined to name the following chap (spoilsports). The man was a thoroughly modern Dad who found time to drop his kids off at school and nursery each day before catching the train to work. Who says Dads can't multitask?

> ### Stuff My Dad Did
>
> 'My Dad somehow forgot I'd changed primary schools and waited for 20 minutes while the whole school filed out past him, leaving me waiting a mile down the road, wondering where he was.'

On this particular morning, our Dad had hopped off his train and was heading into work, a few minutes' earlier than usual. He wondered why: the traffic had been normal, he'd dropped his eldest at school as normal, gone to the station, caught the train...

Hang on, Dad. What about the bit where you drop your other daughter at nursery? Oh dear. Our forgetful father finally remembered he'd driven straight past the kindergarten and had left his one-year-old secured in the station car park. In fairness to our Disastrous Dad, he didn't just try and cover everything up like a Dad normally would when he drops a clanger – as he jumped on the next train back to the station, he frantically rang the police to confess and ask them to attend ASAP. Fortunately it wasn't a hot or cold morning and when Dad arrived the emergency services had already managed to liberate the tot, none the worse for – or even aware of – her ordeal.

> **Patient: Doctor, I keep forgetting things.**
>
> Doctor: How long has this been going on?
>
> **Patient: How long has what been going on?**

DISASTROUS DECISIONS

Aladdin Sane?

In the early years of the 13th century, Ala ad-din Mohammad II had used his muscle to build up quite a little empire – the Khwarezmian Empire to be precise. It might sound like Captain Kirk's latest enemy in *Star Trek*, but it was actually 1.3 million square miles of prime Persian real estate. We don't know whether Ala ad-din was in possession of a magic lamp to help him, but he was probably very keen on passing on his lands intact to his son Jalal.

So when a diplomatic envoy and some merchants arrived from the East in 1218, seeking to establish relations and trade links, Al ad-din suspected a ruse and did what any self-respecting Shah would – he had them executed. This might have been a clever move if the envoy had been sent by a shrinking violet such as myself, but our ruler, in his wisdom, had just decided to pick a fight with Genghis Khan.

The mighty Moghul's next diplomatic mission consisted of 150,000 troops, and within two years the Khwarezmian Empire had been destroyed and Ala ad-din, presumably having mislaid his flying carpet, was dead.

So next time your Dad tells you that all bullies are cowards and you just need to stand up to them, just remind him that Ala ad-din said, 'Genghis Khan't'… but he did!

Stuff My Dad Did

'My Dad drove us down a country lane on holiday that got narrower and narrower until the hedges on both sides were scraping the car. When we finally reached the main road he saw the sign "Unsuitable for motor vehicles".'

Dads' Bad Decisions

You know what they say – if you have to make a 50/50 decision, nine out of ten times you'll pick the wrong one. Here are a few examples of Dads' worst choices:

1. Buying a Betamax video recorder
2. Investing in the Sinclair C5
3. Installing solar panels on his house in Aberystwyth
4. Not turning off the motorway when he sees the 'delays ahead' sign
5. Arriving at a fancy-dress party topless with a pair of Y-fronts strapped across his nipples and saying he's come as a 'chest of drawers'
6. Changing queues at the supermarket checkout
7. Not changing queues at the supermarket checkout
8. Getting a bloke who's 'just got a bit of tarmac left from a job up the road' to re-lay his drive cheap
9. Deciding to drive past a petrol station with the gauge on empty just to save 1p per litre
10. Booking tickets for the semi-finals of any football tournament in the hope of seeing England in them

DAD'S OPEN-MIC 1

A man walked into a pub with a piece of tarmac under his arm.

'Can I have a pint of bitter, please,' he asked, 'and one for the road.'

Where did Herbert go after his home-made space rocket blew up?

Everywhere.

Horace: The trade union has just burned down the match factory.

Herbert: Why did they do that?

Horace: They didn't mean to, but they called a strike...

Son: There's a salesman at the door with a funny face.

Dad: Tell him you've already got one.

What's the difference between a dirty bus stop and a well-endowed female lobster?

One is a crusty bus station, the other is a busty crustacean!

Sick witch: Will I have to stay in bed for long?

Witch-doctor: No, you'll soon be able to get up for a spell.

What happened when the woman backed into a fan?

Dis-assed'er.

What do farmers mend their trousers with?

Cabbage patches.

Horace: It's times like this I wish I'd listened to what my old mum told me.

Herbert: What did she tell you?

Horace: I don't know, I wasn't listening.

Dad: I'm calling to tell you I've just been hit by a piece of falling tree.

Mum: Oh no, are you OK?

Dad: Yes, it was only a leaf.

Horace: How did you get out of Iraq?
Herbert: Iran.

DISCIPLINARY DISASTERS

All the King's Horses Couldn't Get Him to School

Many Dads are pretty laissez-faire when it comes to bringing up their kids. But one or two take things to the other extreme, and go completely over the top. Take the example of Australian Dad, Sam Burt, from Humpty Doo (no kidding!).

Sam's five-year-old son Jack was a bit of a handful, and when he was suspended from using the school bus for five days for throwing an apple core at the driver's head, Dad knew just how to straighten him out.

It was an eight-mile journey from the Burt's remote homestead to the school, and you or I would just have taken the easy option – let Mum drive him to school (we might even have helped by setting the alarm so she didn't forget). But Superdad Sam was made of sterner stuff. So for a week in late 2008, Sam and Jack got up before six o'clock every morning to make the two-and-a-half-hour walk to school.

The internet was impressed at this show of hands-on parenting. One local Mum even set up a Facebook support site, 'The Sam Burt TOUGH LOVE Appreciation and Support Group'. 'We think he's an amazing parent,' she said, and endorsements flooded in, with some calling for him to be Australia's father of the year.

After a week of discipline, Jack was welcomed back onto the school bus. Three stops later he was thrown off for fighting – he later told the *Northern Territory News* all the walking had made him stronger than ever.

More Actual Over the Top Punishments

Misbehaviour: Refusing to take hat off in church.
Reasonable Dad Chastisement: Stabbing.

Misbehaviour: Standing in the way of the TV.
RDC: Shooting in the bum with a BB gun.

Dad: Why are you so scruffy?

Jimmy: Some boy started fighting with me on the way home from school.

Dad: I'm not having that! I'm going to complain to someone. Would you recognise him again?

Jimmy: I'm not sure, but if it helps I've got his ear in my pocket.

Clean Your Room, or Else...

It's surely not unreasonable for a Dad to ask his son to clean his room. And it's also not unusual for the child in question to then throw a tantrum – and in this case also his dinner – in the general direction of the parent.

So in 2009 Andrew Mizsak decided that the appropriate response was a no-nonsense one – he called the police. By the time they turned up at the house in Bedford, Ohio, Dad had calmed down a bit and declined to press charges, which came as a relief to his son Andrew Jr, who was 28 at the time and a wannabe politician (more of a reason to have him locked up, some would say) living rent-free with his parents.

Inevitably though, and luckily for us, the story leaked out, and the Bedford School Board, of which the messy twenty-something was a member, voted to strip him of some of his official duties as a result. A contrite Andrew Jr promised to keep his room tidy in future – though we've all heard that before, haven't we, Dads?

I'll Take That As a 'No', Dad

Joseph Logan loved his American football, and loved his team, Alabama Crimson Tide. In September 2003 he had to endure watching a narrow defeat to Arkansas on TV, not just in overtime, but in *double overtime*, whatever that is. He didn't take it well – voices were raised, doors were slammed, crockery was thrown. The news report doesn't mention falling-down water being involved, but I'm going to hazard a guess that it was.

Joseph's son Seth, obviously not the sharpest tool in the box, decided this would be a good time to ask Dad if he could put his hand in his pocket to help him buy a car. Seth had apparently written off several cars before this, and his request was like a crimson rag to a bull. Joe got his gun, put Seth in a headlock and fired. Fortunately, his aim was no better than the Alabama kicker and he missed. He later said he was only trying to scare his son, but he still ended up being charged with attempted murder.

Maybe the cops were giving him a taste of his own medicine and trying to frighten Joe, because he was eventually allowed to plead guilty to a lesser charge of domestic violence.

Judge: You have been found guilty of assaulting the victim with several guitars. Before I pass sentence, I must check: first offender?

Defendant: No, my Lord. First a Gibson, then a Fender.

Dad Jokes

DEDICATED DISASTERS

Give Me a Kiss, Dad

Some Dads will do anything for their offspring, occasionally taking it to disastrous lengths. Take the example of Donny Denney. Just because Donny Denney Jr was banged up in prison in Colorado it didn't stop him hatching a plan to smuggle some drugs into jail to sell to fellow inmates. And who better to help him than his Dad, Donald Sr.

The first idea was to have a woman visit Don and pass the drugs in a mouth-to-mouth kiss – clever, eh? Unfortunately neither Don knew a single woman willing to help who had a clean enough criminal record to allow her to visit a federal prison.

Never mind, Dad stepped into the breach and volunteered – you can't stop a pa visiting his son, can you? They knew that all phone calls to the prison were monitored, so the Denneys worked out a cunning code to throw the authorities off the scent – they referred to the drugs as 'you know what'. Alan Turing, eat your heart out.

Somehow the geniuses at the prison rumbled the plot and Don Sr was picked up by the FBI on his arrival. They gave him a full body search, which turned up the drugs in a fundamental location – so Don Jr might have been quite happy he wasn't required to kiss his Dad after all.

Stuff My Dad Did

'My Dad once moved along a bench to make room for someone at the other end without realising he was already sitting on the end himself.'

A prisoner's wife wrote him a letter:

Dear Bill, now I need to economise I am going to plant potatoes in that mess of a back garden (though goodness knows how I'll manage to dig it). When is the best time to plant them?

He wrote back:

Dear Joyce, whatever you do, DO NOT dig up the back garden, that's where I buried the loot.

She replied:

Dear Bill, after your last letter 20 policemen came and dug up the whole garden but found nothing and went away.

And received the following:

Dear Joyce, now you can plant your potatoes.

Scout's Honour

It was the Cub Scout's big race of the year, the Pinewood Derby, with around 70 entrants. Don't get too excited – it wasn't being run at the famous film studios, pinewood refers to the material the kids' cars were made of. These are very light – there's a 5-ounce upper limit and strict rules against carrying any liquid to make it heavier.

But the 2004 Derby at Quail Run School, Kansas, had to be postponed when skulduggery was exposed during a practice run as a car overturned and a vial of mercury spilled all over the course. Some dishonest Dad had gone the extra mile by sneaking it on board his son's car to make it handle better.

In the good old days, they'd have just sent for the chemistry teacher to chase the mercury back into a test tube and carried on with the race. This being the 21st century, a lengthy cleanup of the toxic mess ensued, costing some $5,000. When the race was eventually rerun, the son of the culprit was excluded. Bet he was pleased with his Dad.

Large old lady: Excuse me, sonny, could you see me across the road?

Boy Scout: Missus, I could see you half a mile away.

Dad Jokes

What do you call a camel with three humps?

Humphrey!

Happy Birthday, Daddy's Little Princess

Not all Dads' interventions are disastrous – some are just plain weird. Our story starts with a little geographical background…

The territory of Bir Tawil, situated between Egypt and Sudan, has the complex status of *nullius terra*, land that no nation claims. It's basically 800 square miles of desert, a lump of nothing inhabited by no one and so has been the subject of a few cheeky online land grabs from the sort of people who think it's fun to buy land on the moon.

But on 16 June 2014, Jeremiah Heaton of Virginia, United States, did what no one had been bothered to before. He travelled to Bir Tawil, planted a flag and claimed the new Kingdom of North Sudan in person. And he did it all for his daughter Emily, after she asked him if she would ever be a real princess, even planting the flag on her seventh birthday.

Apart from indulging Princess Emily, King Jeremiah has grand plans to develop the fledgling nation as a model scientific base. But although he claims to have established several embassies around the world, as yet no one's returned his calls, and his country remains unrecognised.

On the bright side, though, Sepp Blatter has just announced that the Kingdom of North Sudan has made the short list for the next FIFA World Cup.

DIRECTORIAL DISASTERS

Keep Rolling!

What was family life like before home videos were invented, when hilarious incidents happened just once and were then told and retold to become part of family myth? Now you can't so much as sneeze without it being sent off to *You've Been Framed*, and we've discovered that within every Dad there's a budding Tarantino just waiting to be let out.

Patrick Sweeney, an experienced mountaineer, got a bit carried away in 2014 when he and his kids, 11-year-old Shannon and nine-year-old PJ, were climbing Mont Blanc. They were ascending the mountain's 'Corridor of Death' – I'm not the world's cleverest Dad but I think that would have given me an inkling as to what lay ahead – when a mini-avalanche hissed down the slopes, knocking them off their feet. Being all roped together, Patrick was able to halt their descent with an ice axe, but all the while he kept filming their escapade for posterity (and, of course, YouTube).

The French were not amused (are they ever?). The mayor of the local town said tourists were turning the mountain into an 'amusement park'. Patrick was unrepentant and insisted that, despite the risks, it was better for his kids to climb mountains than be stuck in front of a computer – which seems a very fair point. If the trio had reached the peak, PJ would have broken the record for the youngest ascent of Mont Blanc. And the judgement of the local leader of the mountain guides? 'Zey were trying to break ze record for stupidity.'

Herbert was scaling a mountain when he fell over a ledge and ended up hanging precariously from a small shrub that was sticking out and getting looser by the second.

'Is there anybody there?' he shouted.

'HERBERT!' came a voice. 'THIS IS GOD. LET GO OF THE SHRUB AND I WILL SAVE YOU.'

Herbert paused for a few seconds, then said, 'Is there anybody else up there?'

If You're Shooting, I'm Shooting

A Kentucky Dad of two sunbathing teenage girls was definitely no fan of the cameras one day in 2015. William Meredith took matters into his own hands when he suspected a drone camera of flying over his home to take a peek – he got his shotgun and blew it out of the sky.

The police became involved and everything got a little fuzzy, to be honest, probably much like the pictures taken by the drone, with William claiming he only shot the machine down when it passed directly over his property and the owner of the hi-tech kit, David Boggs, insisting he'd been flying legally and was trying to film a friend's house. Flushed with indignation, Mr Boggs accused the overprotective Dad of being a 'Drone Slayer' – something he'll be quite proud of, I'd have thought.

ANIMAL MADNESS

What do you call an alligator in a vest?

An investigator!

Gators Like Lance a Lot

Lance Lacrosse is a Louisiana tour guide with a difference – and a Dad Disaster waiting to happen. When he goes to work in the morning, his kids must wonder how much of him will come back that night.

Lance works in the local swamps, showing tourists the wildlife, with particular emphasis on the alligators. He isn't exactly your Attenborough-style guide, whispering, 'Now, if we all sit here quietly for three hours we might catch a glimpse of one of these magnificent beasts as it drifts past in the distance…'

Lance has more of the typical Dad approach. If you want to see a gator, obviously you just throw a chicken into the water to entice them, then to keep them interested you jump in the swamp with a load of marshmallows.

Lance isn't daft enough to feed them by hand – he doesn't want to lose any fingers. No, obviously he puts the marshmallows between his lips and lets the sweet-toothed reptiles take them directly from his mouth. One of the greedy gators has got so accustomed (or perhaps attracted) to Lance that he lets the guide re-enact Patrick Swayze's famous lift from *Dirty Dancing*. Then Lance raises one of the brute's front legs to wave goodbye to the visitors.

In 2014, film of Lance's exploits made its way online; sadly, his bosses took a dim view of his alligator antics and put the block on him. Spoilsports.

Snake's Alive!

This really is a disastrous story of a Dad who reached the end of his tether, but it does have a happy ending... sort of.

Towards the end of the 20th century in Darwin, Australia, poor old Gordon Lyons was in a right state. A messy divorce had left him fighting for custody of his kids. After drowning his sorrows, he and a friend were driving through the outback when they spotted a deadly brown snake. Gordon persuaded his friend to stop so he could catch the snake; the venomous creature promptly bit him and Gordon popped it into a sack.

It was widely reported that Gordon was so stupidly drunk that despite losing the first round to one of the most dangerous animals on the planet he decided to go back for more and stuck his arm in the sack. In Lyons v. snake there was only going to be one winner, old brownie biting Gordon a further eight times. He very nearly died and surgeons had to amputate Gordon's badly damaged arm. What a twit, eh?

But in 2009, Gordon related a slightly different version to the *Northern Territory News*. It hadn't been drunken bravado that caused him to tackle the snake, but depression – it was a grisly suicide attempt.

The good news is that Gordon is now, despite the loss of his arm, in a more contented place. And for any Dad out there tempted to wrestle a venomous viper, here is the voice of experience: 'I wouldn't do it again,' he admits.

Stuff My Dad Did

'My Dad thought it would be cool to use a skateboard to walk the dog – the sound of the scraping wheels scared the dog, who took off, pulling Dad into a hedge.'

DANCING
DISASTERS

Dad Dancing Reimagined

Dad Dancing, it seems, has become the hot topic *de nos jours*; there's no getting away from it. Someone should write a book about it.*

And I seem to recall that another recurring theme of Dadship is just how flippin' embarrassing they are to their offspring. Well, a trio of London daughters turned the tables at the tail-end of 2014. Rosie Heafford, Alexandrina Hemsley and Helena Webb devised a show and workshop experience called, naturally, *Dad Dancing*. Its aim was to 'reimagine relationships between fathers and their children' through dancing. Well, quite. I can't imagine it going down a storm at the Cleckheaton Working Men's Club, but apparently it's the sort of thing they like in Battersea.

Rosie, Alex and Helena thought it would be a great idea to showcase 'the care, the embarrassment and love' that fatherhood involves, all wrapped up in the ethos of 'care, bravery and inclusivity'. It was so inclusive, they included their Dads, Adrian, David and Andy, in the show, strutting their stuff to a variety of music and, according to the website, 'reclaiming "Dad Dancing" from the cynics'.

Cynics! I do hope that barb wasn't aimed at me, ladies.

* *Dad Dancing* by Ian Allen, Portico Books, £7.99 (26 used from £0.01).

Ladies and Gentlemen, We Have a Winner!

Step forward – or maybe sashay in a ridiculous mince – Conrad Gillespie, crowned the 2015 World Dad Dancing Champion at the second annual Dadfest event in Devon. Well done, sir!

The Vine-al Countdown

Stuff My Dad Did

'My Dad fractured his sternum breakdancing in front of all my friends.'

When presenter and Egghead-tamer Jeremy Vine was unveiled as a contestant on *Strictly Come Dancing* 2015, he told Chris Evans, 'I've got to start dancing properly. I can't go into the Dad Dancing.' He decided there was only one thing stopping him: he just needed to, in his words, 'identify my left foot'.

Well, there was great news for Jeremy in September when he made his *Strictly* debut and it was obvious that he hadn't just found *one* left foot, he'd got two of them! Not even the talents of Karen Clifton could paper over the cracks in Jeremy's technique. The panel's resident baddie, Craig Revel Horwood described it as 'flat-footed', 'disjointed' and 'disconnected', and informed viewers that he'd seen a 'bizarre bottom wiggle' going on.

Jeremy obviously has hidden talents with the ladies, though, because fellow judge and former prima ballerina Darcey Bussell said it was 'strangely fabulous'.

He proved a hit with viewers though and, despite being described by Craig as dancing 'like a stork struck by lightning', surfed a tidal wave of sympathy votes all the way to mid-November, when he finally landed in the dance-off and inevitably became the seventh celeb to be booted out. Poor Jezza missed the prestigious Blackpool *Strictly* by just one week!

Anyway, it's a good excuse to ~~steal~~ showcase an Edinburgh Fringe award-winning joke from his brother Tim.

Tim Vine's joke:
I decided to get rid of my Hoover… well, it was just collecting dust.

Dad's version:
I bought my wife a new bag and belt last week… well, she's been complaining about the Hoover for ages.

Stuff My Dad Did

'My Dad was a fireman and went to the station's Christmas fancy-dress party in drag. With a certain inevitability there was a callout during the party and Dad turned up at the fire in his uniform but also with full make-up and a pair of large gold hooped earrings.'

Horace: I got so cross yesterday trying to fit all the clothes in my wardrobe.

Herbert: You need to go to some hanger management classes.

Dad Jokes

FASHION DISASTERS

Dad, What Are You Wearing?

If there's one thing that's guaranteed never to go out of fashion, it's having a go at Dad's appalling dress sense. In 2015 there were a plethora of fashion stories all lining up to make fun of Dads. For instance, what looked to me like a highly practical and stylish sandal with Velcro strips was immediately dubbed the 'Dad Sandal' – 'Do you dare to wear it?' asked the *Daily Telegraph*. GAP launched a very dashing item – 'Dad shorts'; 'wide-legged jeans – precisely the sort of thing your Dad wears on holiday', said *The Guardian*. In other words, cut-off jeans, except Dads are too clever to pay GAP prices – we just take a pair of scissors to an old pair that's worn through at the knees (no grunge look for us, thank you very much).

In August 2015, self-styled fashionista, hipster and father-to-be Robin Sherwood agonised, again in *The Grauniad*, 'Does fatherhood really mean I have to become "dadcore" – wearing clothing that is comfortable, with no real regard for fit or appearance?' I think I speak for all Dads when I say that I wish Robin all the best as he enters fatherhood, and look forward immensely to inspecting his wardrobe in five years' time.

Dad Jokes

Why do golfers wear two pairs of trousers?

In case they get a hole in one!

What's brown and slippery?

My slippers.

Dad's Fashion Falsisms

Your typical Dad is often to be found uttering truisms that, while they might apply to normal people, are so inappropriate for him we'd have to call them 'falsisms'. Here are five of the best.

1. Everything comes back into fashion eventually
2. Black looks good on anybody
3. Stripes make you look thinner
4. You can carry off any look with enough confidence
5. Good jeans never need washing

Stuff My Dad Did

'My Dad was given a pair of "sandal socks" – white socks with the image of a sandal on them – for a joke. Obviously he now wears them *with* his sandals!'

DISASTROUS DITTIES

Tomorrow I went to the pictures,
I found a front seat at the back,
I bought a plain cake with some currants in,
I ate it and gave it them back.

Roses are red,
Violets are blue,
Most poems rhyme,
But not this one.

Said Hamlet to Ophelia,
I'll draw a sketch of thee,
What kind of pencil shall I use?
2B or not 2B?
(*Spike Milligan*)

Little birdie in the sky
Dropped a present in my eye,
And I thought as he flew by,
I'm just glad that cows don't fly!

I eat my peas with honey,
I've done it all my life,
It makes the peas taste funny,
But it keeps them on the knife.

DAD'S OPEN-MIC

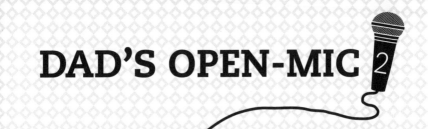

Horace: I've trained my dog to say his own name.

Herbert: That's fantastic. What's his name?

Horace: Woof.

Why was the origami expert useless at poker?

He kept folding all the time.

Arial, Palatino and Comic Sans go into a bar.

The barman says, 'We don't serve your types in here.'

Horace: I went to the opera for the first time last night.

Herbert: Was it good?

Horace: It was OK, but they don't like it when you join in.

Why didn't it hurt when the man got hit with a can of Coke?

It was a soft drink.

Hotel guest: I've just put some money in your snack dispenser and all that happened was it said, 'I don't half fancy your wife.'

Receptionist: I'm sorry sir, that machine's out of order.

A man robbed a music shop yesterday and got away with the lute...

Horace: I think I'm in a football marriage.

Herbert: How do you mean?

Horace: Well, every couple of hours it all kicks off.

What do hills listen with?

Mountaineers!

Cow: How come when all us cows were blown over by that terrible storm last night, you bulls just swayed a bit but stayed on your feet?

Bull: Surely you know, we bulls wobble but we don't fall down.

Sheila: Would you like to see where I was tattooed?

Frank: I certainly would!

Sheila: Well, keep your eyes peeled, it's that place on the corner of the high street next to Poundland.

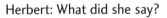

Horace: I gave my wife a ring on our anniversary.

Herbert: What did she say?

Horace: She asked me where the hell I was ringing from.

What do steam trains listen with?

Engineers!

DISASTROUS EXAMPLES

Fags Very Much!

Most Dads try to be a good influence on their kids and spare no expense indulging their whims. And many parents will say that you never know what they'll enjoy unless you give them the chance to try different things; hence little Jemimas and Jaspers being exposed to violins, French horns and harmonicas, and encouraged to try durian fruit, asparagus and goats' cheese. Personally, I'd draw the line at Woodbines, though.

Not so Mohammed Rizal of Indonesia. When his son Ardi was 18 months old, Mohammed thought it would be a good idea to see if he fancied a crafty fag – who knows, perhaps he was working on the old theory, 'Make them smoke when they're young and they'll turn against it.' By 2010, when Ardi was two years old, he was so sick of them that he had a 40-a-day habit. If he didn't get his fix, he'd throw a tantrum, screaming and banging his head, and his distraught Mum would give in. Who said indulgent, liberal parenting was the preserve of the West? His Dad took a more phlegmatic approach: 'He looks pretty healthy to me,' he was reported as saying.

By the end of 2013, however, news from Indonesia was good-ish. Ardi had cracked his tobacco habit – but was now reportedly hooked on junk food.

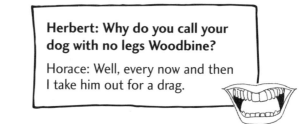

Herbert: Why do you call your dog with no legs Woodbine?

Horace: Well, every now and then I take him out for a drag.

Dad Jokes

Insanity is hereditary – Dads get it from their kids.

I'm a Belieber... in Genetics

Justin Bieber has had his brushes with the law down the years – his alleged misdemeanours include driving under the influence and drag racing (at the same time), assaulting his driver and egging his neighbour's house, and in June 2015 he pleaded guilty to charges of assault and careless driving when he trashed a photographer's van.

Mind you, it seems he's only following the example of his Dad Jeremy, too, as the website Celebuzz! (my favourite) reported in January 2014. He was apparently banged up for 90 days in 1997 for assault, and then served later terms for breaking the terms of his probation. He was again charged with assault in 2003, but the charges were dismissed.

And why am I picking on the poor old Biebers out of the countless examples of Dads leading their sons astray? Surely not so I can make the obvious joke that Justin hasn't just got one criminal record, he's got loads!!

Anyway, just when you thought Justin's Dad couldn't be any more of an embarrassment to his son, in October 2015 he was posting toe-curling tweets on the subject of nude photos of his offspring that leaked online. I won't go into detail here; suffice to say he declared himself a 'proud daddy'… Ugh!

DENTAL DISASTERS

Time of Take-off – Tooth Hurty

Dads are notorious for doing daft things with potentially disastrous consequences. OK, at the time of writing I don't have names to back up the following tale, but there is definitely video evidence (thank you, YouTube). In September 2015 footage was posted to the video-sharing site of a Dad who took a modern approach to removing his daughter's first wobbly tooth.

Attaching a tooth with string to a door handle in the time-honoured fashion of *The Beano* is so 20th century – this Dad decided to move with the times and bring in the drone. With one end of some dental floss tied to the little girl's precarious premolar and the other to a piece of kit that looks more high-spec than an Apollo lander, it's hard to decide who was more excited, the patient or the amateur drone-tist. To be fair to Dad, there's no indication that she was an unwilling participant, more like a chip off the old block.

It would have suited the purposes of this book (while being very unfair on the tot in question) for Junior to have been dragged along the ground when the contraption took off, her tooth stubbornly clinging to her gums, the drone's motors burning out and the machine itself crashing to earth, preferably knocking out Dad as it did so. Sadly – I mean, fortunately – and against all common sense, it all went without a hitch; the wobbler came out as clean as a whistle and even landed a few feet in front of the little girl on the grass so she'd have something for the tooth fairy.

Stuff My Dad Did

'My Dad still insists that when I woke to find him with his hand under my pillow the morning after I'd lost a tooth, he was just checking to see if the tooth fairy had been… that was 20 years ago.'

Patient: Ever since I've given up cigarettes I've felt like an ATM.

Doctor: Don't worry, they're just withdrawal symptoms.

Dad Jokes

What does the Dentist of the Year win?

A little plaque.

Why did the Buddhist refuse an injection before he had a filling done?

He wanted to transcend dental medication.

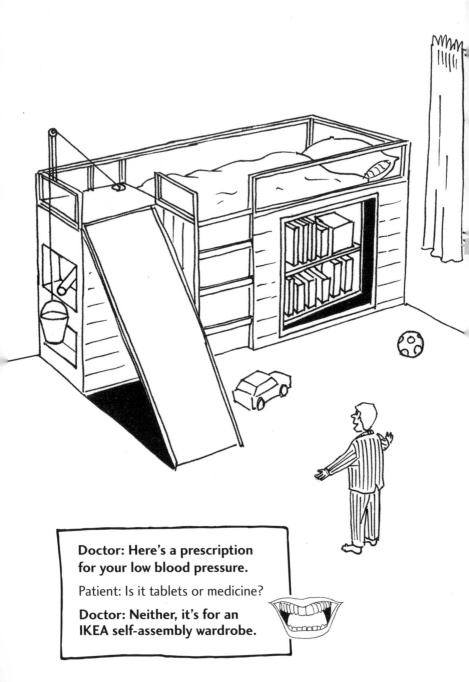

Doctor: Here's a prescription for your low blood pressure.

Patient: Is it tablets or medicine?

Doctor: Neither, it's for an IKEA self-assembly wardrobe.

GIVING DADS A GOOD NAME

Eric Wasn't Idle

There's nothing more disastrous for normal Dads than when the occasional Superdad comes along to show us all up. In August 2014 Eric Strong posted a video to YouTube showing how he helped his son's transition from a cot to a proper bed by buying a bed from IKEA and modifying it slightly. Well, actually he bought two beds from IKEA to give him a bit more scope, so he could add a slide to get out of bed… and a specially designed marble run… and a rope and pulley system to retrieve the marbles… oh, and a secret room underneath the bed with colour-changing lights and a spy-hatch for looking out from… and did I mention the magic book in the bookcase that operates the door to the secret room?

When I bought my son a bunk bed I 'modified' it by putting the ladder on the wrong side, breaking two of the slats holding the mattress up and taking a gouge out of both my hand and the wall when a screwdriver slipped. Thanks, Eric. On behalf of all of us underachievers, I'd like to suggest Eric keeps his achievements to himself in future.

World's Best Father

Have you ever wondered who the *worst* father is to possess one of those hilarious and obligatory mugs with 'World's Best Father' emblazoned on it? I certainly have, and I wonder if Alice Bee has.

Alice was born in December 2010, and it wasn't long before her father, photographer Dave Engledow, was taking endearing family snaps of him and Alice sharing those precious father-daughter moments.

1. Dave drinking his coffee while Alice hoovers (he is considerately lifting his feet so she can vacuum thoroughly)
2. Alice holding a nail as Dave prepares to whack it with a hammer
3. Alice sitting inside a hollowed-out pumpkin as Dave sculpts it with a large carving knife
4. Alice ironing as Dave reads his newspaper
5. Alice sitting atop a lit barbecue preparing burgers for her impatient Dad
6. Dave driving at top speed to work (late) while Alice sits in her car seat on the roof

… and many more, all featuring Dave proudly holding his 'World's Best Father' mug.

When I showed these pictures to my wife she had the temerity to suggest that some of these pictures had been staged, if not digitally altered. Frankly, the idea that such a fine, upstanding example of Dad-dom would stoop to such measures just to flog his calendars is one I find astonishing in its cynicism. I invite you to look up Mr Engledow on the internet and judge for yourself.

Stuff My Dad Did

'My Dad cut the end off his finger while sawing a piece of wood.' 'And my Dad decided to chop down a tree in the garden half an hour after giving blood and then wondered why he fainted!'

Patient: Doctor, I've just swallowed a roll of film, will I be OK?

Doctor: We'll just have to wait and see what develops.

What did Cinderella sing when she left Boots?

'Some day my prints will come.'

Dad Jokes

Chemist: Here are your photos, would you like the negatives?

Customer: Yes please.

Chemist: OK, they're quite blurred and you need to pay more attention to your composition.

Stuff My Dad Did

'My Dad went to dive through a door dressed as Superman to surprise us kids. The door he thought was open was latched and he knocked himself out.'

FAMILY PLANNING DISASTERS

Top 15 Fertile Fathers

No matter how good a Dad you are, it's possible to spread yourself too thin. Once you get into double figures the problems really start to mount up, so what disastrous Dads these must have made, those who, according to Wikipedia (so it must be true), fathered a hundred or more children. It would have been a lot less if it had been them changing the nappies, I'll tell you that for nothing. So, let's start our countdown…

 Fath-Ali Shah Qajar (1772–1834) Shah of Persia from 1797 until his death, he was also famous for having a very long beard.
Number of kids 108-plus

 Mienh Trin (19th century) See no. 10.
Number of kids 114

 King Saud of Saudi Arabia (1902–69) Not a great king (extravagant and wasteful, he was forced to abdicate in 1964), but good at begetting.
Number of kids 115

 Misheck Doctor Nyandoro (1955–present) This Zimbabwean farmer is reportedly trying to solve Zimbabwe's population crisis single-handedly. With 18 wives to date, he told the Zimbabwe *Herald* in 2014 that he had no plans to stop, so expect to see the self-styled 'Dr Love' climbing the charts soon.
Number of kids 128

Winston Blackmore (?–present) The leader of a breakaway Mormonist sect in Canada, where he's been in a long-running criminal case over polygamy charges.
Number of kids 130-plus

 Minh Mang (1791–1841) Isolationist Emperor of Vietnam with very strict views on the missionary position – he executed them! Two of his sons also make this list, Mienh Trin at no. 14 and Mien Tham at no. 9.
Number of kids 142

 Mien Tham (19th century) See no. 10.
Number of kids 144

 Ramesses II (13th century BC) One of Egypt's greatest Pharaohs and the inspiration for Shelley's famous poem 'Ozymandias'. When he died in his nineties, this Daddy became a Mummy, which was dug up in 1881.
Number of kids 156

 Jack Kigongo (1909–2012) Lt Kigongo of Uganda married 20 times, and left 11 widows when he died in 2012. At one point it's said of the local school population of 130 children, 80 were Jack's.
Number of kids 158

 Ancentus 'Danger' Akuku (1916–2010) Nicknamed for his knack of attracting the ladies, Kenyan 'Danger' Akuku married over a hundred times and divorced on 30 occasions; he had to build his own church to accommodate his growing family – presumably his favourite song was 'I Do, I Do, I Do, I Do, I Do'.
Number of kids 160-plus

Ibrahim Njoya (1860–1933) This Cameroonian king succeeded his father, Nsangu, to the throne at a young age, but apparently had to wait to take over officially because an old enemy of his Dad's wouldn't release Nsangu's head, which was considered inauspicious.
Number of kids 177

 Sobhuza II (1899–1982) Sobhuza was the King of Swaziland for 82 years, a world record, having succeeded his father at the age of four months. His Dad, Ngwane V, died while taking part in the ritual *incwala* dance – so if you had any doubts about the dangers of Dad Dancing… you have been warned.
Number of kids 210

 Augustus II (1670–1733) Also known as Augustus the Strong, this King of Poland liked to indulge in a bit of fox-tossing (it's as cruel as it sounds). Not being a polygamist like many in this list, Augustus accumulated mistresses on a grand scale and had only one legitimate son.
Number of kids 365-plus

 Ismail Ibn Sharif (1634?–1727) King of Morocco and known as 'the Bloodthirsty', it seems Ismail was a nasty piece of work who had thousands of slaves and thought nothing of having them tortured and killed for trivial reasons. Makes your Dad look a bit better, eh?
Number of kids 867

 Genghis Khan (1162–1227) Who's the Daddy? Yes, it's the towering Mongol leader whose armies swept across Asia crushing all before them. His most famous descendant is probably Kublai Khan, but seeing as a 2003 genetics paper estimated that 0.5 per cent of the men in the world share his genes, there's a 1-in-200 chance it could be me!
Number of kids 1,000-plus

DAD'S DAFT XMAS CAROLS

We Three Kings of Orient are,
One in a taxi, one in a car,
One on a scooter pipping his hooter,
Doesn't get very far.

We Three Kings of Leicester Square
Selling ladies' underwear,
So fantastic, no elastic,
Seven and six a pair.

While shepherds washed their socks by night,
All hanging on a line,
The Angel of the Lord came down
And said those socks are mine.

While shepherds watched the box by night
Enjoying BBC,
The Angel of the Lord came down
And switched to ITV.

Good King Wenceslas looked out
On his cabbage garden,
Bumped into a Brussels sprout
And said, 'I beg your pardon.'

TRANSPORT DISASTERS

Where's Wally?

Wally*, from Texas, was on vacation with his family in 2012, a good ol' American road-trip – I hope for Wally's sake it was one of those cavernous Winnebagos that you can imagine getting lost in, rather than a VW campervan.

You see, after they'd stopped at a filling station in Tennessee, to refuel themselves and the van, Wally somehow got left behind. When he realised, he rang everybody in the van… but no one responded. Eventually someone suggested using Facebook to contact the fugitives and Wally finally managed to alert his family – now 100 miles away – to his absence.

Now I can't be the only one smelling a rat here. Surely Wally's family, having put up with him from Texas to Tennessee, were making a run for it, desperate for a few hours without suffering his ZZ Top CD or listening to his awful jokes. Picture the scene:

Wally Jr: He's not here – floor it, Ma.

Ma: OK, here goes. Y'all turn your phones off, y'hear.

[Two hours later…]

Wally Jr: Aw, shoot, Ma, he's used Facebook – now I kin't pretend I ain't done seen it.

*Wally is a pseudonym… but then you knew that.

Stuff My Dad Did

'My Dad wound up the electric window on his car with his hand still sticking out of it and took his fingernail off.'

Don't Listen to Your Dad – At Least Not Yet

In April 2015 Joseph Forren of Connecticut received a very helpful text from his Dad: 'Don't drink and drive.' Joseph was apparently reading the text as he crashed into a truck and banged his head. Thankfully no one was seriously hurt, but when police arrived they tested Joseph and found he was twice the legal alcohol limit. They also found the text message. (Another text arrived while the police were on the scene, saying: 'I know you're drunk, but at least answer me.' It's not thought this was admissible as evidence.)

Horace: Hello, who's there?

Herbert: I've been trying to phone you all morning, what are you doing?

Horace: From the look on the examiner's face, I'm failing my driving test.

Customer: Can you let me have a pair of windscreen wipers for my Nissan Micra?

Halford's assistant: OK, that seems like a fair swap.

DAD'S OPEN-MIC 3

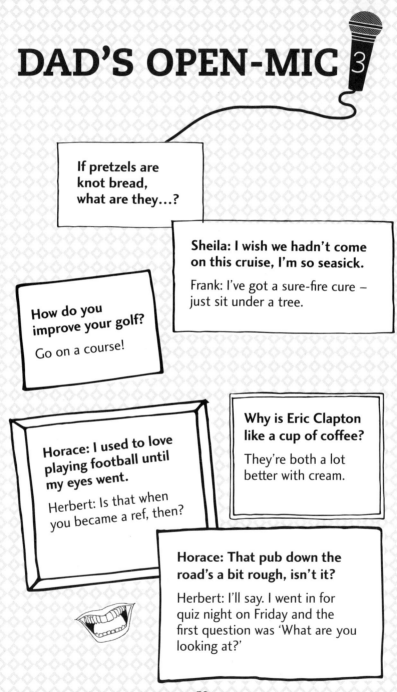

If pretzels are knot bread, what are they...?

Sheila: I wish we hadn't come on this cruise, I'm so seasick.

Frank: I've got a sure-fire cure – just sit under a tree.

How do you improve your golf?

Go on a course!

Horace: I used to love playing football until my eyes went.

Herbert: Is that when you became a ref, then?

Why is Eric Clapton like a cup of coffee?

They're both a lot better with cream.

Horace: That pub down the road's a bit rough, isn't it?

Herbert: I'll say. I went in for quiz night on Friday and the first question was 'What are you looking at?'

An elderly man was being very hesitant at a T-junction and a long line of traffic built up behind him. Eventually the chap in the car behind got out and went up to him.

'Look,' he said, 'the sign says Give Way, not Give Up!'

Wear a watch and you'll always know the time – wear two and you'll never be sure…

What always sleeps with its shoes on?

A horse!

Dad: Mum says you've got something to tell me.

Jimmy: Um, yes. Me and Johnny were having a weeing competition against the outside wall to see who could go the highest. Mum came out and saw us – she hit the roof.

Dad: Wow! Did she win?

Why was the little ant confused?

All his uncles were ants!

Bank robber: Give me £20,000 or you're geography.

Bank teller: Don't you mean history?

Robber: Don't change the subject!

MOTOR DISASTERS

'Eads'll Roll for This Mistake

Who is the Daddy of mass-produced cars, the man who brought motorisation to millions? That's right, Henry Ford. So what better way to pay tribute to the master of the black car himself than to name a new model after his son, Edsel. What could possibly go wrong?

Well, it turns out, just about everything. It was launched with great pomp in 1957, even having its own TV show to sound the fanfare. But its styling was so hideous even the Americans were turned off it. Despite having numerous innovations like warning lights and a rolling speedometer – it even had seatbelts, for heaven's sake – the Edsel was seen as too expensive for its market and failed to catch the public's imagination. Production problems meant that some cars left the assembly line with unfitted parts left in the boot to be added by the dealers, who sometimes 'forgot' to do this.

After dismal sales figures the model was ditched in 1959. Ford lost $350 million on the project – the equivalent of $2.8 billion in today's money – and any automotive flop for years to come was nicknamed an 'Edsel'. The only surprising thing is that more daft Dads didn't buy this four-wheeled disaster.

What's in a Name?

Car manufacturers are always desperate to come up with snappy new names for their latest models, but these can sometimes go wrong. By all accounts the AMC Gremlin wasn't a bad car, but the idea of naming it after all those annoying hard-to-find faults was surely a mistake. And was it silly or spookily prescient of Studebaker to call its new 1920s model the 'Dictator', just as Mussolini and Hitler were flexing their muscles? Much better to call in Dad and let him have a go at naming some cars with his awful puns.

Stuff My Dad Did

'My Dad once put a gallon of oil in his car engine instead of a pint and then wondered why blue smoke was pouring through the dashboard.'

1. Ferrari Sajolligoodfella
2. Ford Orconvertible
3. GM Crops
4. Datsun Cogs*
5. Audi Do
6. Fiat Atickets
7. Honda Horizon
8. Leyland El*
9. Morgan Freeman
10. Mini Haha

*See old Dad joke about it 'raining Datsun cogs'.
**Guaranteed to annoy the neighbours.

Dad Jokes

Jimmy: Mum, what happens when a car gets all old and rubbish and keeps breaking down?

Mum: Someone sells it to your Dad.

Horace: I've just seen an AA van go past and the driver was crying his eyes out.

Herbert: Sounds like he's heading for a breakdown.

Stuff My Dad Did

'My Dad parked his car on the beach and the tide came in and swallowed it up.' 'And my Dad parked his new car in a busy car park and had to ring home to ask its colour and registration so he could find it.'

DIETARY DISASTERS

Curry On Dieting

According to a recent study (where would we be without them), new fathers tend to gain weight compared to their childless counterparts. I'm not sure that can be the entire explanation for how Mike Snell, a Dad from Chester, got up to 24 stone, but his way of getting rid of the fat is a novel one, and probably not recommended by experts.

Mike starts every day with a chicken vindaloo and also allows himself to cram in whatever else he fancies up until 10am. Then he has nothing else all day until a little snack in the evening. Like most Dads, he doesn't like being told what to do (or what not to eat), so thought he'd give his unusual diet a whirl – well, probably several Hazelnut Whirls, a few Mars Bars and a KitKat (nothing After Eight, though).

Mike was always snacking as he delivered goods to various supermarkets in his area, but he reckons his technique takes away any cravings he has for the rest of the day; with no changes to the amount of exercise he takes, he's lost over 10 stone in less than a year.

You certainly can't 'takeaway' from Mike's achievements – and if you tried he'd probably tell you it was naan of your business.

Indian takeaway knock-knock joke:

Knock, knock.

Cumin.

Why are you throwing that rice at me?

I thought you wanted a pilau fight.

A brain walks into a pub and asks for a pint of beer.

'I'm not serving you,' says the barman, 'you're out of your head already.'

Shut Up and Drink Your Greens

And now a story to have any Dad queueing up for his five a day. Richard Hood and Nick Moyle – a.k.a. the Two Thirsty Gardeners – were two graphic designers who decided to give cider-making a go. Apples are good for you, aren't they? The results weren't half bad and so they branched out into that old home-produced staple, rhubarb wine. After a few glasses of that their imaginations ran riot and soon they were developing recipes for rhubarb cocktail, chicory beer and plum liqueur. They proved so popular the chaps brought a book out last year, *Brew It Yourself*. Mind you, as most recipes involve waiting anything from a week to a few months, I think I'll stick to my own healthy instant smoothie produced with a bottle of Guinness, half a dozen carrots and a blender.

Stuff My Dad Did

'My Dad poured a barrel of neat industrial perfume over our drive to disguise the smell of a delivery of manure. It made the pong ten times worse and people were crossing the road to avoid us for months.'

MUM'S CORNER

Dum and Mad

Dads have to take a lot of stick for being generally daft and causing disastrous mishaps. But what about Mums? Research for this book brought it home to me that they can be just as bonkers as Dads, though I expect they'll blame us. As someone once said, 'Mum on her own is fine, but add Dad and you get Dum and Mad.' So here are a few examples of when Mums acted more like Dads.

Take the Night Bus

American Mom Roselean Walker took a laissez-faire approach to child-minding any Dad would be proud of. In December 2005 she took her 11-year-old son to the local multiplex to see the latest *Harry Potter* film. Not being a fan of the young wizard, she quite reasonably went to another screen to watch something else with her boyfriend, what Dad would call a 'proper film', i.e. one lasting about an hour-and-a-half. As *Harry Potter* belongs to the modern trend of film-making (a three-hour film must automatically be twice as good as a 90-minute film), when she came out of her screening she got fed up of waiting for Junior and headed home – if a 12-year-old Harry can kill an obelisk or an asterisk or whatever,* surely her kid can make it back home?

Apparently not. The police called Roselean next morning, saying they'd got her son if she'd like to collect him. She suggested it would suit her better if the cops dropped him off, whereupon they got a bit shirty and demanded her immediate attendance. Mom turned up in a foul mood issuing threats of lawyers and all sorts. In the end she needed one – she was charged with assaulting a police officer and endangering a child's welfare.

*Editor's note: *It was a basilisk.*

Don't Slope Off – Pay Up!

When five-year-old Alex of Cornwall was invited to a birthday party at a dry ski slope at the end of 2014 his parents said he could go. Then, on the day, they realised they were double-booked, and Alex missed the party. Dad Derek had lost the invitation with the contact details (a Dad losing something – surely not!) and so couldn't send apologies.

You might expect that what followed would be the typical school-gate embarrassed mumbled apology and gritted-teeth 'Don't worry about it' from the Mum in question. But no. Our Mum, Julie, asked the school to pop another letter into little Alex's school bag. Was it an ostensibly caring but ultimately sarcastic note, expressing the hope that Alex wasn't 'ill' on the party day? No. It was an 'official' typed invoice from Julie for £15.95 for a 'no-show'.

Well, Derek refused to pay and – predictably, in this day and age – it all kicked off on Facebook, the Twitterati lined up to have their say and even the national media took an interest. Julie expressed the opinion that ,'The amicable way round this I believe would be to pay me the money,' but the chances of it being settled amicably by then were pretty nonexistent.

The ski slope, very sensibly, distanced themselves from the row, saying: 'We would like all our customers to know that this invoice has *nothing* to do with Plymouth Ski and Snowboard Centre.'

Never mind, Alex – maybe Julie will ask you again next year…

Dad: I threw some snow at your Mum this morning.

Son: What happened?

Dad: She didn't catch my drift.

What do you call a wizard with a secret plan?

Harry Plotter.

MORE CRIMINAL DISASTERS

Irish Stew in the Name of the Law

And that punchline to a terrible knock-knock joke means it's time to have another look at some disastrous Dad encounters with the boys in blue. Strangely enough, they all seem to originate from North America... there must be something in the water.

The Curse of Modern Technology

In May 2005 a daft Dad accidentally locked his keys inside his Cadillac late one night. What a twit. Still, at least he didn't do something really stupid like locking his two-year-old son inside as well... Oh... I see...

Not to worry, his Caddy was fitted with the latest Onstar emergency button, one push of which alerts the police and leads them to your location, in this case an Albuquerque trailer park.

For some reason Dad wasn't keen on his lad pushing the button, so of course Junior duly pushed it, and when the local deputies arrived they found Dad trying to persuade his son to unlock the door manually and a few other chaps hanging around whistling innocently. After releasing the kid via the Onstar's automatic unlock system, the cops, on a roll and feeling lucky, decided to search a nearby trailer and discovered 1,700 pounds of marijuana – you could say they hit the jack-'pot'.

Dad was arrested along with the other men, and probably reflected that it would have been a lot cheaper to have just smashed the car window.

Stuff My Dad Did

'My Dad once set off the security
alarms at the Scottish Parliament
with a packet of polos.'

Keeping It in the Family

In July 2008 father and daughter Benjamin and
Stephanie Martinez both went to work at the same pizza parlour in
Denton, Texas.

That sounds nice, doesn't it?

But while Stephanie worked behind the counter, her Dad had a
more unorthodox role in mind. Armed with a toy gun, and disguised
with wig and glasses, he threatened and punched a cashier and
attempted to rob the place. When this employee made a spirited
counterattack, Benjamin's disguise was dislodged, which was when
Stephanie realised for the first time who the miscreant was.

'Don't hit him again, that's my Dad,' she is reported to have
shouted in dismay. As if that wasn't a big enough shock for the
poor girl, she later discovered that the getaway car was being
driven by her husband, with her mother keeping him company.

'I thought I was robbing a convenience store,' said Benjamin
in his defence. Taking into account his criminal record, the
prosecution asked for a life sentence, but the judge took pity on
him and sent the 41-year-old down for a mere 60 years.

The pizza parlour's owners believed Stephanie when she
insisted she knew nothing about the planned heist and even
offered to keep her on but, understandably, she couldn't face going
back. Dads really know how to embarrass their kids,
don't they?

Look What I Did, Daddy…

Back in 2005 in Canada, a toddler was punching random numbers into a phone keypad and came up with 911. Cue blues and twos dashing round on a mercy mission, where they found a completely unfazed one-year-old and, more significantly, her Dad, who was in hiding after breaking his parole.

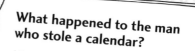

Dad Jokes

What happened to the man who stole a calendar?

He got 12 months!

Sheila: Frank, wake up, there's a burglar in the kitchen eating that pie I made for dinner.

Frank: Which shall I call first, police or ambulance?

I'm a Disastrous Dad, Get Me Out of Here

It was Father's Day 2003 and former security guard William Kline of Des Moines, Iowa, got his old handcuffs out to show his son, ten-year-old Brian. In a touching reaffirmation of the strong bond between father and son, little Brian cuffed himself to Dad. All great fun and very touching, but eventually it was time to take the cuffs off and go and have some dinner. Where's the key, Dad?... Dad?

Oh dear. When William left his job he'd kept the shiny, funny handcuffs, but had completely forgotten where he'd put the key. Cue an embarrassing phone call to the local nick to see if they could separate father and son. Officers duly turned up and released the pair; everyone had a jolly good laugh about it and the policemen left.

This would be a good Dad story if it ended here, but it gets even better.

The cops returned to their car and, as per protocol, ran William's details through the police computer. Oops! Two outstanding warrants for minor misdemeanours showed up, and within minutes Dad was back in handcuffs and on his way to the station.

Even though he spent the rest of Father's Day in jail before being bailed, Dad was understanding about the whole thing. He even forgave Brian: 'When I got home I gave him a kiss right away to let him know there were no hard feelings.'

He was probably more careful about where he put his keys from then on though.

DISCOVERY DISASTERS

Greater Love Hath No Man...

… than he lays down his son's health for his research project.

Irukandji Syndrome is a nasty disease, causing back pain and nausea, and in extreme cases can bring on cardiac arrest. In the early 1960s Dr Jack Barnes of Cairns, Australia, had a pretty good idea it was passed on through the sting of a tiny jellyfish, now named *Carukia barnesi* in his honour. To catch one he sat on the seabed for some time in a weighted diving suit.

The suspect specimen procured, Jack now had to test his theory, which he did by letting it sting him. He was a good scientist, though, and realised that a single case study was insufficient to draw conclusions from, so he used it to sting his nine-year-old son and, for good measure, a passing lifeguard. Pretty soon all three were suffering varying degrees of discomfort and were rushed to hospital, but happily they all recovered after 24 hours.

So Jack had his theory proved right, his son (I suppose) shared in the kudos of the jellyfish carrying his name, but goodness only knows what the lifeguard got out of it, apart from an unexpected day off.

Dad Jokes

What happened to the hen who laid the world's biggest egg?

She won the Pullet Surprise.

A blonde and a professor were on a train journey together and the professor thought he'd have some fun.

'Let's play a game,' he said. 'We'll ask each other questions, and every time you don't know the answer you give me £5, and every time I don't know the answer I'll give you £50.'

The blonde accepted and the professor asked her, 'What's the element symbol for gold?'

She admitted she didn't know, gave him a £5 note, and he told her it was Au. Then she asked, 'What's got 11 legs, three heads and four stomachs?'

The professor thought for ages but had to admit he was stumped, and handed over £50. The blonde accepted it and went back to her magazine.

'Well,' said the professor, 'What *has* got 11 legs, three heads and four stomachs?'

The blonde gave him a £5 note.

What happened to the man who invented the door knocker?

He won the No-bell Prize.

A chemistry student went into the chemists' bar with his history student friend, asked the chemist barman for some H_2O, and was served a glass of water.

His friend, not wishing to appear ignorant, said, 'I'll have some H_2O too.'

It nearly killed him.

Why can't you trust atoms?

They make up everything.

DISTRACTED DISASTERS

Making a Grab for It

Those arcade machines where you have to use a crane to grab a toy are really annoying. Every time you think you've got one it slips out and you have to start again. You spend enough money on the game to buy one of the toys ten times over. Wouldn't it be great if you could just climb inside and take your pick?

That's ridiculous, though, because if you were small enough to climb inside you'd have someone responsible with you keeping an eye on you, like your D—

Oh. Right.

In 2004, when Frank Novotny of Sheboygan, Wisconsin, went with his little Timmy to the Piggly Wiggly supermarket and needed to make a call on a nearby pay phone, he just assumed his seven-year-old would be content to look at the stuffed toys behind the glass. Well, stuff that, thought Timmy, I'm going in.

When Dad turned round from the phone all he could see was a pair of legs sticking out of the 8 x 11-inch opening – the body was past the point of no return. Reports don't record how much time or money Dad spent trying to grab Timmy with the crane – I'd have given it a good few goes, personally. Anyway, firefighters were called but, perhaps wisely, and considering Tiny Tim seemed perfectly happy in among the toys, decided against setting about the machine with axes and instead carried it to the back of the store while they waited for a locksmith to drill out the mechanism and open the front of the game.

About an hour later Timmy was free, and left the store with his Dad – Mr Piggly Wiggly didn't even give him a toy for his trouble.

DRIVING DISASTERS

It's All Right, Dad, We'll Get the Bus

You might think your Dad is a disaster on four wheels, and wonder how he ever passed his test. But it could be worse. Take the example of Stuart MacNamara up before the magistrates on driving charges in Swansea in 2001.

Back in those days, it wasn't strictly speaking illegal to use a mobile phone while driving, so the fact that this Dad of four drove through a red light while yakking away on his mobile meant the authorities could get him for jumping the lights and 'not having proper control of his vehicle'. To compound matters, this Dad was also over the drink-drive limit, despite protesting that, although he'd had a skinful, it had been 14 hours ago.

This was all bad enough but, to put the icing on the cake, as Stuart was tipsily careering through a red light while deep in conversation with a phone pressed to his ear, he was steering with his elbow. He had a very good reason for doing this, mind – he only had one arm and was driving an unadapted vehicle.

Stuart had lost his forearm in an accident and, in a typical example of misplaced Dad confidence, decided he could drive perfectly well without it. The courts disagreed and banned him from driving for 18 months.

'My Dad drives along listening to Radio 3, conducting an imaginary orchestra as he goes. Goodness knows what other motorists make of it – they probably think he's gesticulating wildly to them.'

Dad: I think I've flooded the carburettor.

Mum: You don't know a thing about cars – what makes you think it's flooded?

Dad: I've just driven into the canal.

Dad Jokes

Horace: My wife wants me to buy her something that will go from 0–200 in a few seconds.

Herbert: Why don't you get her a set of bathroom scales?

DAD'S OPEN-MIC 4

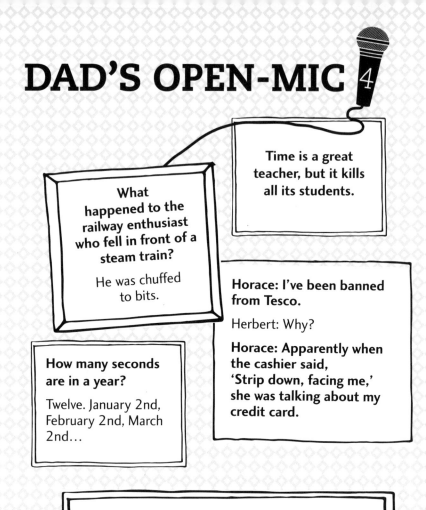

Time is a great teacher, but it kills all its students.

What happened to the railway enthusiast who fell in front of a steam train?

He was chuffed to bits.

Horace: I've been banned from Tesco.

Herbert: Why?

Horace: Apparently when the cashier said, 'Strip down, facing me,' she was talking about my credit card.

How many seconds are in a year?

Twelve. January 2nd, February 2nd, March 2nd…

A man was in the supermarket checkout queue with a massive trolley full of stuff when a little old lady came up behind with him holding a pint of milk and a small loaf of bread.

'Is that all you've got, love?' asked the man.

She said that it was.

'You'd better join another queue then, because I'm going to be ages…'

Bigamy is the only time when two rites make a wrong.

Diner: Why can I hear the Red Flag coming out of the kitchen?

Waiter: Don't worry, sir, that's just the Commie chef.

Horace: I'm going to suggest to my boss we open a farm shop.

Herbert: Are you sure that's a good idea – you do work at the sewage farm.

Sheila: I set myself a goal this year to lose 10 pounds.

Joyce: How's it going?

Sheila: Well, I've only another 15 to go!

A doctor went into his local and ordered his usual, which was a special walnut daiquiri the barman had created for him. On this occasion the barman was out of walnuts, so grabbed whatever was to hand and hoped his customer wouldn't notice. But he did.

'Hey,' he said, 'what's this?'

'Oh, sorry,' said the barman, 'that's a hickory daiquiri, Doc.'

MORE DIY DISASTERS

Shorten Sweet

Aussie Brad Shorten was a brickie's labourer who'd taken a nail gun home for a bit of DIY. Some mates had come round, the conversation turned to construction-site accidents and Brad decided to show them how mishaps could occur. He disconnected the nail gun from its compressor to disable it, and put what he thought was now an empty tool to his temple.

He was wrong on both counts.

He pressed the trigger and, though he felt no pain, a little red dot appeared on his head. There had been enough pressure left in the gun to fire the inch-and-a-quarter nail that now lay recessed inside Brad's skull. Because he couldn't see it, Brad thought it was just a scratch.

But when he started to feel a bit woozy, his 13-year-old son Nathan – who had obviously inherited his brains from his Mum – insisted they call an ambulance. When Brad arrived at the hospital he asked the nurses for a pair of pliers so he could remove the offending nail himself. The nurses declined his request; a good job too, because according to the neurosurgeon, Dr Kevin Siu, that would have been 'the worst thing to do'. (I think the doc was just being selfish – once people realise it's OK to perform DIY brain-surgery with a pair of pliers, chaps like Kevin will be looking for a job.)

Instead they sawed off part of Brad's skull and carefully removed the nail. Afterwards he was suitably contrite, telling the Victoria *Sunday Herald Sun*: 'I did a very stupid thing.'

'My Dad got hot tar all over his hands while roofing a church hall. He went to use the toilet and got his hand stuck in an awkward place, and the vicar had to help set him free!'

'My Dad built a kitchen table that wobbled so much he nailed it to the floor – when he sold the house the table had to stay behind.'

Horace and Herbert were working on a building site digging a trench. Horace took a careless swing of his spade and lopped off Herbert's ear.

'Don't worry, Herbert,' he said, 'I'll help you look for it.'

After a minute of searching through the mud, Horace exclaimed, 'Here it is.'

Herbert came over and had a look. 'That's not it,' he said. 'Mine had a pencil behind it.'

Dad Jokes

HISTORIC DISASTERS

It Seemed Like Such a Good Deal

Tsar Alexander II of Russia – a prodigious father who had eight legitimate children and at least another seven born on the wrong side of the blanket – probably felt pretty pleased with himself when he managed to get $7 million from the United States for some frozen, desolate land thousands of miles from Moscow that was proving very hard to hold on to strategically anyway.

The Yanks weren't universally impressed either. After the 1867 purchase had been negotiated by US Secretary of State William Seward some dubbed it 'Seward's folly' or 'Seward's icebox'. In his defence, it was pointed out that although he had essentially bought an icy wilderness, it was a very, very big icy wilderness – the price worked out at a measly two cents per acre.

And when gold was discovered in the new Territory of Alaska towards the end of the 19th century, it became apparent that the Tsar had, in typical Dad fashion, sold it at the bottom of the market. Not that it bothered either man by then. Seward died in 1872 and Alexander II was finally assassinated (after several previous attempts) in 1881.

Nearly a century later, in 1959, Alaska finally became a state of the USA in its own right.

Jane: Do you or Mum know the most northerly of the United States?

Dad: Erm, I'll ask her.

Jane: Gosh, Dad, you're cleverer than I thought.

> **Horace: Hello, Herbert, I'm stuck on a ferry in the straits outside Istanbul and will be late for work.**
>
> Herbert: What do you want me to do?
>
> **Horace: Can you tell the boss for us?**

Did You Lock the Door?

Constantinople had a very long history under different names. It started life as Byzantium, in around 660 BC, before Constantine the Great established the city he modestly named after himself about a thousand years later. It retained that name for well over another thousand years, and now we know it as Istanbul.

But it was another Constantine, the 11th, who concerns us, and he wasn't even a Dad – unusually for rulers of the time, he had no kids. What he did have, in 1453, was a big problem in the shape of an invading Ottoman army. (I thought the Ottomans would have spent all day lounging around on the sofa, but apparently not.) It wasn't necessarily a disaster, though. Constantinople was a very well-defended site. After a seven-week siege beside the Bosphorus, the Ottomans threw everything into a final assault, and it was nip and tuck until a vital moment.

We'll never know for sure who it was who left the little postern gate – the *kerkoporta* – open which allowed the attacking force to enter the city and raise their flags, causing mass panic and the eventual defeat of the defenders. But I like to think it was a Dad who had just popped out to get a paper and couldn't believe what he found when he came back.

Knock, knock.

Who's there?

Armageddon.

Armageddon who?

Armageddon out of here!

DELUSIONAL DISASTERS

The End Is Nigh

Phew! I'm writing this entry on 8 October 2015, and I've just had a narrow escape (as have you) because, according to one Dad, the world was supposed to end yesterday.

Chris McCann, who runs the eBible Fellowship based in Philadelphia, confidently predicted that all the people who had confidently predicted that the world would end in March 2012 (like Chris McCann's eBible Fellowship) as well as all the people who had confidently predicted that the world would end on 21 May 2011 (like a certain Chris McCann) were wrong. He had it on good authority that 7 October was now *the* date by which everyone should have sorted out all the rubbish in their garage and made sure they had clean underwear on for the rapture. This was – obviously – because it was 1,600 days since the Chris-endorsed Harold Camping (see Top Ten Doomsday Dads overleaf) 'judgement day' of 21 May 2011, during which time the Almighty had been sifting and sieving the worthy from the unworthy.

Chris's Facebook page, which somehow seems to have survived the Apocalypse, states that he worked at 'God' and studied at 'Bible'; his employer seems to have been feeding Chris duff information. Chris resurfaced to admit with good grace that he accepted the overwhelming evidence that the world had not ended on schedule but he was still confident that it would happen… 'soon'.

In fairness, it's not as though Chris is the first Dad to have seen imminent Armageddon as a good excuse for not mowing the lawn or painting the bathroom.

Top Ten Doomsday Dads

1 **Hilary of Poitiers (c. 310–c. 367)** Sometimes referred to as the 'Hammer of the Arians' (which, being an Aries myself, puts me right off him), this bishop denounced the Emperor Constantius II as the Antichrist.
Predicted end of world: 365

2 **Arnaldus de Villa Nova (c.1240–1311)** Physician, astrologer and alchemist, he died in a shipwreck.
Predicted end of world: 1378

3 **Thomas Muntzer (c.1489–1525)** German preacher with too many enemies – he took on both the established church and Martin Luther. He led a peasants' uprising and met a predictably grisly end as a result, executed after being tortured.
Predicted end of world: 1524–26

4 **Christopher Columbus (c.1450–1506)** A Dad who needs no introduction, and who features elsewhere in these pages (see Directional Disasters, page 88), he wrote a *Book of Prophecies* towards the end of his life.
Predicted end of world: 1656

5 **John Napier (1550–1617)** An ostensibly sensible (and brilliant) mathematician who discovered logarithms and invented a calculating device known as 'Napier's Bones', this Scotsman had a fascination for the Book of Revelation. He died of gout.
Predicted end of world: 1688

6 **Jacob Bernoulli (1655–1705)** Another mathematician, but this one's interest was comets, specifically the one he predicted would return in 1719 and destroy the Earth.
Predicted end of world: 5 April 1719

7 **William Miller (1782–1849)** An American preacher who along with his followers, the imaginatively named Millerites, had three goes at predicting the Second Coming; the passing of the final date came to be known as 'The Great Disappointment' – though personally I'd describe any postponement of Judgement Day as 'The Huge Sigh of Relief'. *Predicted end of world:* 21 March 1844; 18 April 1844; 22 October 1844

8 **Wilbur Voliva (1870–1942)** Wilbur was a dedicated Flat Earth-ist who was convinced the sun was only 3,000 miles away and just 32 miles across because, he reasoned, who would be daft enough to build a house in Illinois and put the lamp to light it in Wisconsin. When you put it like that, I suppose he has a point. *Predicted end of world:* 1923, 1927, 1930, 1934, 1935

9 **Herbert Armstrong (1892–1986)** Founder of the Radio Church of God, Herbert insisted he was God's selected representative on Earth, Christ's apostle, which presumably explained how he justified travelling by personal jet – I expect it symbolised Jesus' entry into Jerusalem on the 1st-century equivalent, a donkey. *Predicted end of world:* 1936, 1943, 1972, 1975

10 **Harold Camping (1921–2013)** The Daddy of them all, and an inspiration for Chris McCann (see page 85). Harold had a few stabs at predicting the rapture in 1994, then tried again in 2011. The day after the May deadline passed, he confessed he was 'flabbergasted', but said he wouldn't be returning any money to those who sent it to him in the anticipation that they'd no longer need it (what Harold thought he needed it for is less clear, though I have my own theories). *Predicted end of world:* 6 September 1994, 29 September 1994, 2 October 1994, 31 March 1995, 21 May 2011, 21 October 2011

DIRECTIONAL DISASTERS

Satnav Maria! I'm Lost

By the end of the 15th century all people of science knew that the world was round. So what would be great would be if you could sail across the Atlantic straight to India instead of going by the lengthy overland route.

Our reckless Dad without a map, Christopher Columbus, decided he was the man to achieve fame and fortune by sailing his ship, the *Santa Maria,* west to the Indies. But he made two big mistakes. Firstly, he believed some erroneous 1,300-year-old figures that said the planet's oceans only covered about a third of the circumference of the Earth. He then compounded the error by mixing up his Arabic and Italian miles, which any fool knows are quite different. All this meant that he believed the distance from the Canary Islands (the last westward point he could restock his vessels) to Japan (the furthest point known to the east and hence the first place he knew he would find more stores) to be about 3,000 miles. This was a long way, but just about doable. The problem for Columbus – and what many sceptics suspected – was that the actual distance between the Canaries and Japan is more like 12,000 miles, an impossibly long sea voyage at the time.

So naysayers of Columbus's plans didn't think he was going to sail off the end of the world – they just thought he'd die of thirst.

Of course, in a typical example of the dumb luck that Dads sometimes enjoy when they get lost, someone had thoughtfully placed the Americas slap-bang in the place where Columbus expected India to be, which is why the islands of the Caribbean are known as the West Indies.

> ## Stuff My Dad Did
>
> 'My Dad once drove into next door's drive by mistake and didn't realise until he wondered why his house key wouldn't work.'

I'll Risk It

In 2008 lorry driver Steven Ablett missed his son's 18th birthday party because he listened to his satnav instead of his common sense. While making a delivery in Cornwall he obeyed the machine and ignored the sign that said 'Not suitable for heavy vehicles' – at least we now know that 17½ tons is officially heavy.

The lane got narrower and narrower and when Steven reached a tight bend he realised the game was up. Unfortunately he couldn't reverse back up the road due to a very muddy surface, and had to spend the night in his truck, blocking what was a useful short cut for locals. By the next morning rain had washed away enough of the mud for him to be able to reverse back up the lane, but it wasn't soon enough for him to get back to Cambridgeshire for his son's big day.

'I probably shouldn't have ignored this sign,' he admitted.

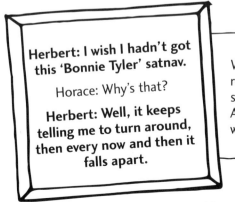

Herbert: I wish I hadn't got this 'Bonnie Tyler' satnav.

Horace: Why's that?

Herbert: Well, it keeps telling me to turn around, then every now and then it falls apart.

West Yorkshire Police have reported that all their satnavs have been stolen. A spokesman said they were still looking for Leeds.

DAD'S OPEN-MIC 5

Checkout lady: I'm going to bet that you're single.

Man at checkout: I suppose it's the ready-meals for one that give it away?

Checkout lady: No, you're just really ugly.

A man was on a plane and got up to use the toilet. When he came back someone was sitting in his seat.

'I'm sorry,' said the man, 'I thought you'd got off.'

Horace: I've just read a book about Stockholm Syndrome.

Herbert: What was it like?

Horace: Well, at first I hated it but by the end I thought it was great.

How do you kill a blue elephant?
With a blue elephant gun.

How do you kill a white elephant?
Hold its trunk until it turns blue, then use your blue elephant gun.

Horace: Do you know that Eskimos eat whale meat and blubber?

Herbert: Well, so would I if I had to eat whale meat.

Customer:
I'm building a barbecue, and I'd like 10,000 bricks, please.

B&Q assistant: That's far too many for a barbecue, sir.

Customer: Not if you live on the ninth floor.

Jimmy: What's the name of that dinosaur that's really big, enormous, massive, gigantic...?

Jane: A thesaurus?

I'm not a bad ventriloquist, though I say so myself.

Horace: My wife's just gone to play percussion in an orchestra in Australia.

Herbert: Woollongong?

Horace: No, you idiot, a metal one.

Surgeon: You need a brain transplant, Mr Smith, and with modern technology we are now able to offer you one. We can give you a doctor's brain for £10,000, a surgeon's brain for £50,000 or a footballer's brain for £100,000.

Mr Smith: Why is the footballer's brain so expensive?

Surgeon: Well, it's never been used.

NAMING DISASTERS

We Are Not Amused

Can there be a more momentous decision a Dad gets to make than to name his offspring? There are some weird examples nowadays, but in these days of equality the blame can be shared between Mum and Dad. Not so in Victorian times, when surely the man of the house would have had to shoulder the responsibility completely.

In 2015 the genealogy firm Fraser and Fraser published a list of really weird Victorian names they'd come across during their researches. They even included the original certificates so no one could accuse them of making it up. Opposite are ten of the best:

Stuff My Dad Did

'My Dad was so discombobulated after I was born he exited through the entrance of the hospital car park and nearly hit an ambulance coming in.'

Dad Jokes

Horace: Before I marry Doris I need to get something off my chest.

Herbert: What's that?

Horace: A tattoo that says 'I love Mary'.

92

1863 **Leicester Railway Cope** Anticipating the Beckhams by over a century, this lad was apparently born (not conceived, alas) in a railway carriage.

1870 **One Too Many Gouldstone** Perhaps a permanent reminder of the circumstances of the poor boy's conception.

1871 **Friendless Baxter** What better start to school life could a boy wish?

1876 **Windsor Castle** Son of William Castle, his mother's maiden name was King!

1879 **Clifton Antivaccination West** Goodness knows what the equivalent would be today, probably Charlie Tax The Rich Smith or Eric Save The Pound Brown.

1883 **Ann Bertha Cecilia Diana Emily Fanny Gertrude Hypatia Iug Jane Kate Louisa Maud Nora Orphelia Quince Rebecca Starkey Teresa Ulysis Venus Winifred Xenophen Yetty Zeus** And if you're wondering where the 'P' was, her surname was Pepper. And there was probably another Q – behind Dad at the register office!

1885 **King Arthur Johnson** No delusions of grandeur whatsoever.

1886 **That's It Who'd Have Thought It Restell** For some inexplicable reason he later changed his name to George.

1892 **Mineral Girl Waters** Dad missed a trick with the addition of the middle name, I reckon.

1899 **Time Of Day** Son of Thomas Day, at least this selfish Dad was unlikely to give him away to anyone.

Do You Mind If I Just Call You Nick?

Nicholas Barbon (1640–98) was an influential figure in 17th-century London; he was a physician, an economist (an early proponent of free-market theory in fact) and, particularly in the aftermath of the Great Fire of London in 1666, a major house-builder. He also helped to develop the insurance industry, particularly in respect to fires, and he ended up a Member of Parliament.

Although he traded as Barbon, his actual surname was Barebone, and he had a famous father, Praise-God Barebone, after whom the English Parliament of 1653, the Barebone's Parliament, was named. With a Dad called Praise-God (and apparently an uncle called Fear-God), you might think Nicholas had got off lightly.

Not a bit of it. His full name was Nicholas Unless-Jesus-Christ-Had-Died-For-Thee-Thou-Hadst-Been-Damned Barebones. But you can just make the cheque out to Nicholas Barbon.

Why, Son, Why?

In 2013 an 18-year-old from Florida attempted to murder his father by stabbing him in an apparently motiveless attack. The 54-year-old Mr Blanchard recovered, and is still trying to puzzle out what he could possibly have done to make his son, Bamboo Flute Blanchard, want to attack him.

Dad Jokes

Teacher: What's your name?

New boy: Billy, sir.

Teacher: Well, I call all my boys by their surname, what's your full name?

New boy: Billy Sweetie, sir.

Teacher: Very well, sit down, Billy.

Teacher: Simon, can you say your name backwards for me?

Simon: No, mis.

Horace: I'm fed up with being called Horace Smelly, I'm going to change my name.

Herbert: That's a good idea, what to?

Horace: Well, I quite like the sound of Harold Smelly.

DOZY DISASTERS

If a Thing's Worth Doing, It's Worth Doing Quickly

Your average Dad won't hesitate to get out of a chore if he possibly can, and if he can't, then his motto tends to be: *Valet facere quod, facere valet cito* (see above).

And to back this up, Bill Gates of Microsoft has apparently said that if you've got a difficult task, you should hire a lazy person, because they'll find an easy way round it. And remember, while the early bird gets the worm, when it comes to mousetraps it's the second mouse that gets the cheese. Here are some examples of Dads putting this into action.

Buss Stops When He Gets Home

In 2003 there was an attempt to tag father-of-three Chris Buss as the laziest man in Britain, just because when he's at home he's waited on hand and foot by his wife Paula. But Chris gets up at *half-past four* every morning to go to work – OK, he has to get up that early apparently so that Paula can wash and blow-dry his hair – and he doesn't get in until 7pm. Now unless he has a secret double life and is spending all day in the pub and at the pictures, I don't call that lazy, it's just being well organised.

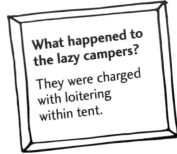

What happened to the lazy campers?

They were charged with loitering within tent.

Vortigern Should've Thought Again

Fifth-century Briton King Vortigern was said to have been fed up with having to fight off the Picts and Scots that came raiding over his borders. He'd heard that there were a couple of brothers called Hengist and Horsa who, together with a load of Angles and Saxons in what is now Germany, simply *loved* fighting. They couldn't get enough of it. What a great idea it would be, thought Vortigern, to invite the H boys over to do the dirty work for me.

So he did, and they did. And once they'd beaten up the Picts and the Scots, they took a look around and thought to themselves, 'This is actually a very nice place. And as it seems we're the only beggars here who know one end of a sword from another, we think we'll stay.'

Not only did they stay, they invited a few thousand of their mates over as well, and before you could say 'Vortigern, you idiot', the Britons were being ruled by the Saxons, who stayed in charge until 1066.

First woman at bus stop: That council workman over there hasn't done a thing all the time we've been standing here. He must be the laziest man in town.

Second woman: Actually, that's my husband.

First woman: Oh, I'm sorry.

Second woman: *You're* sorry…

Dad Jokes

Pyle's Crowned Great North Bum

In 2008 Newcastle's Century Radio decided to run a light-hearted competition called the Great North Bum – their thought being that in a rush to glorify and laud all those sweaty articles who take part in the Great North Run every year, the prime of North East manhood had been overlooked. So just who was the laziest man in the region?

In the end it was no contest. Karl Pyle nominated his Dad Kevin, who every morning gets Karl up at five o'clock to help him walk their dog, a bull mastiff called Bruce. Now admittedly Bruce is a big dog and according to Kevin he 'pulls a lot', but why on earth does it take two people to walk him?

Stuff My Dad Did

'My Dad spent 80 quid on a pair of snazzy yellow trainers, only for us to point out when he got home that they had "LADY RUNNER" emblazoned on the side.'

Well, one morning when Kevin got up to find it was raining, he hit upon a brilliant idea. Rousing Karl, he made his son drive the car slowly round the block while Kevin sat in the passenger seat with his arm out of the window holding Bruce's lead as he trots alongside. 'He really enjoys it,' said Kevin, who is obviously an expert in canine interpretation.

I'm not sure how much use he got out of his prize though – a session with a personal trainer and a month's membership to a local gym.

MORE DISCIPLINARY DISASTERS

Sentenced to Watch TV

It seems to me that all the examples of inspirational Dads dishing out novel sanctions seem to come from across the pond. There must be something about the can-do attitude over there that encourages Dads to think not just outside the box, but on top of the roof (metaphorically speaking – I don't recommend anyone pops their recalcitrant kids on the roof as a punishment). So all rise for our first example of innovative American Dad discipline.

C-Span is an American television network, roughly equivalent to our BBC Parliament. What do you mean, you haven't watched BBC Parliament? It's brilliant, it covers the House of Commons, the Lords, Select Committees and in the autumn, for a special treat, the party conferences.

When his daughters come home after the time laid down, Steve Kissing from Cincinnati makes them watch five minutes of C-Span for every minute late they are, and then write a report on it. Blimey, he's good.

First hippie: Turn the TV on, man.

Second hippie: Hey, TV... I love you!

Stuff My Dad Did

'My Dad thought it would be "fun" to shoot a pellet gun near Mum to scare her as she bent over – he was a much better shot than he thought and hit her right in the backside!'

Note to Self – Set Facebook to Private

In 2012 Tommy Jordan did a nice Dad thing for his 15-year-old daughter Hannah – he upgraded her laptop. OK, he's an IT chap, but it still took him six hours and cost him $130. Hannah duly took to Facebook to post a message, 'To my parents'.

But rather than thank her Dad for the trouble he'd gone to, she had a foul-mouthed rant over all the chores she had to do, signing off, 'when you get too old… and you call me asking for help, I won't be there'.

It was pretty tame stuff, really, the kind of venting teenagers have done to their mates since time immemorial – you can imagine a young Elizabeth Tudor complaining to her chums that 'it is so unfair that I've been, like, cut out completely, just because Mum got her head chopped off' – but putting it on the internet is the equivalent of Lizzie daubing it in foot-high letters all over the walls of Greenwich Palace. Young Hannah forgot the cardinal rule that you have to be very, very careful with anything you post online. Sure enough, Dad got to see it.

If I tell you that, having thought long and hard, Tommy reached for his gun, you might start to be concerned. Don't worry. Tommy got his gun, set his video rolling, took careful aim, and shot the laptop nine times. Then he posted the footage to YouTube, where it's fair to say it went down a storm.

MORE ANIMAL MADNESS

Who's a Pretty Boy, Then?

The monk parakeet, also known as the Quaker parrot, is a pretty little bird, native to South America but living feral in several other areas, including the United States.

When James Martin heard that a neighbour of his wanted to get one for his girlfriend, but was having trouble raising the $100 for a captive one, he had a great idea – just down the road from him were plenty of the birds nesting in the grounds of the Florida Power Corp. He offered to go down there with his son and nab a baby specimen for his mate.

The neighbour, 18-year-old Damion – which with hindsight was probably a bad Omen – decided to come along as well. He had the bright idea of bringing along a pole to dislodge the hatchlings from their perch.

Now, a responsible adult might have had something to say at the prospect of poking around a 230,000-volt substation with a 7-foot-long metal pole, but James was (still is, I hope) a Dad. He probably just said something like, 'That'll be handy, why didn't I think of that?' He also ignored the 6-foot fence and the welcome signs saying 'No Trespassing' and 'Danger, High Voltage'.

What even James couldn't ignore was the shocking way Damion lit up like a Christmas tree when his pole touched a vital component, because the current hit him as well. Both men were taken to hospital with nasty burns; James Jr, thank goodness, was unhurt.

Stuff My Dad Did

'My Dad went to Dudley Zoo and mistook the chair lifts for pelicans. It may be many years ago now, but that's something we'll never let him forget!'

A magician on a cruise ship had a parrot who, whenever the tricks were being done, would squawk out, 'It's up his sleeve!' or 'It's in his hat!'

Anyway, one night the ship sank, and the sun rose to find the magician and his parrot clinging to a piece of wreckage, with nothing and no one to be seen anywhere.

After about four hours, the parrot finally said, 'OK, I give up. What have you done with the ship?'

Horace was walking down the street when he came across Herbert running towards him.

'A lion's escaped from the zoo,' panted Herbert.

'Which way did he go?' asked Horace.

'You don't think I'm chasing it, do you!' Herbert replied.

DAD'S OPEN-MIC

Driver: What am I supposed to do with this speeding ticket?

Policeman: Hold on to it, and when you get four you get a bicycle.

Horace: Howard's getting married on his 100th birthday to a 20-year-old model.

Herbert: What are you giving him?

Horace: About two weeks...

When is a door not a door?

When it's ajar!

Why is bowling the quietest sport?

Because you can hear a pin drop!

Today is the first day of the rest of your life... but so was yesterday, and look how that turned out.

Horace: I still remember my mother-in-law's last words.

Herbert: What were they?

Horace: 'What are you doing with that pillow?'

Bill: I know I've not been the best husband up to now, but I've decided to make you the happiest woman in the world.

Joyce: Where are you going to live?

Why did King Kong climb the Empire State Building?

He wouldn't fit in the lift.

Horace: Why haven't you done up the laces on your left shoe.

Herbert: Well, it said on the bottom, 'Taiwan'.

What's a balloon's least favourite music?

Pop!

Sheila: Frank decided as I'm so unpredictable he'd buy me a mood ring that would tell him how I'm feeling.

Joyce: Does it work?

Sheila: Sort of. When I'm calm, like now, it's green, and when I'm cross it leaves a big red mark on his forehead.

FICTIONAL DISASTERS

Literature's Worst Dads

Heathcliff A brooding, romantic bad boy in *Wuthering Heights*, but what a rotter he is to his sickly son Linton, forcing him into an unwanted marriage. Boo!

King Laius 'I told him,' said the Oracle, 'I told Laius if he ever had a child he'd be killed by him, but would he listen?' Of course not, this is a Greek tragedy. Laius had a cunning plan to get round it, and when his son Oedipus was born left him on a hillside to die. A kindly old shepherd intervened and Laius' fate was sealed.

Michael Henchard The title character of Thomas Hardy's *The Mayor of Casterbridge*; in his youth Henchard embarked on his own version of *Bargain Hunt* and auctioned off his wife and daughter at a country fair.

Craster This nasty piece of work from George R.R. Martin's *Game of Thrones* lives in a forest with his daughters, whom he marries and forbids to leave him. When they have sons they are left out in the forest for the spooky 'Others' to take. Nice.

Dr Evil The anti-hero of the *Austin Powers* film series, his poor son Scott never stood a chance in such a dysfunctional environment. When Scott asks his Dad why he ran out on him, Dr (not Mr – 'I didn't spend six years in evil medical school to be called Mr') Evil replies bluntly, 'Because you're not quite evil enough.' Even when Scott points out his Dad's stupid mistakes he gets rebuffed – Dr Evil much prefers his cloned creation, Mini-Me.

FINAL DISASTERS

Famous Last Words

OK, I've cheated a bit on this one – but what better way to close the book than with a round-up of a favourite Dad topic, famous last words. After all, if death isn't a disaster, what is? Throughout the disastrous events recounted in the preceding pages, I've done my very best to make sure that the protagonists were bona fide Dads, but I have to confess that I'm not 100 per cent sure that *all* the men quoted on the pages that follow were Dads, and I have a sneaking suspicion that the couple of women quoted weren't Dads either. Equally, I have an inkling that not all these last words are totally reliable. Ah well.

Consider this final entry a disastrously misleading and inaccurate – but hopefully entertaining – conclusion to a book of Dad disasters.

**Horace:
I know that wherever my Dad is, he's looking down on me.**

Herbert: I didn't know he was dead.

Horace: He isn't, he's just a real snob.

Wise Guys

Some people can't stop cracking jokes even when they're at death's door.

'Yeah, country music.'
Drummer Buddy Rich when asked by a nurse, 'Is there anything you can't take?'

'Why should I want to talk to you? I've just been talking to your boss.'
Playwright Wilson Mizner on his deathbed when a priest said, 'I'm sure you want to talk to me.'

'Leave the shower curtain on the inside of the tub.'
Hotelier Conrad Hilton, asked if he had any last words of wisdom.

'Surprise me.'
Comedy legend Bob Hope, when his wife asked where he wanted to be buried.

'This is no time to be making new enemies.'
Author and philosopher Voltaire, on being asked by a priest if he renounced Satan.

'Die, I should say not, dear fellow. No Barrymore would allow such a conventional thing to happen to him.'
Actor John Barrymore.

'Better not. She'd only ask me to take a message to Albert.'
Former PM Benjamin Disraeli declining the offer of a deathbed visit from Queen Victoria.

'Die, my dear doctor? Why, that's the last thing I shall do.'
And another PM on his last legs, Viscount Palmerston.

'This isn't Hamlet, you know. It's not meant to go in the bloody ear.'
Sir Laurence Olivier to a nurse who spilled water as she attempted to moisten his lips.

Wise Gals

And it's not just the men who have left us smiling, as these examples prove.

'Am I dying or is this my birthday?'
Lady Nancy Astor.

'A woman who can fart is not dead.'
Comtesse de Vercellis, after letting go of an impressive deathbed bottom-burp.

Dad Jokes

An ice-cream man has been found in his van covered in hundreds and thousands.

Police believe he topped himself.

At Herbert's funeral the pallbearers trip up the steps and drop the coffin. The lid dislodges and they hear a little moan. Herbert's alive! They manage to revive him and he lives for another five years before dying 'again'.

This time, as the pallbearers carry the coffin in, Herbert's wife says, 'Just watch out for them steps!'

Phlegmatic Characters

Not all condemned prisoners turn into a gibbering wreck like Jimmy Cagney. Some of them see it as their last chance to make a mark.

'Bring me a bullet-proof vest.'
James W. Rodgers in front of a firing squad when asked if he had any last requests.

'Well, gentlemen, you're about to see a baked Appel.'
George Appel before going to the electric chair.

'Hey, fellas! How about this for a headline? "French Fries!"'
James French, ditto.

'Gents, this is an educational project. You are about to witness the damaging effect electricity has on Wood.'
Frederick Wood, ditto. (What is it about that electric chair?)

'I am starting to believe you are not intending to count me among your friends.'
Playwright Pedro Munoz Seca, about to be shot by firing squad in the Spanish Civil War.

'Is it safe?'
Poisoner William Palmer before stepping on the gallows trapdoor.

'This hath not offended the king.'
Thomas More moving his beard out of the way of the executioner's axe before it descended.

Stupid Last Words

Just as the commentator's curse never fails ('Alistair Cook is playing beautifully today and looking impregnable... oh, he's bowled him!'), the minute these words left the lips these people were as good as dead.

'I'll show you that it won't shoot.'
Singer Johnny Ace, while playing with a pistol and pointing it at his head.

'They couldn't hit an elephant at this distance.'
Major-General John Sedgewick at the beginning of the Battle of Spotsylvania Courthouse.

'But how the devil do you think this could harm me?'
Philosopher Denis Diderot's words to his wife when she warned him against overeating.

'Don't worry, it's not loaded.'
Musician Terry Kath, pointing a gun at his head (he was wrong!).

'The Lord God is my armour.'
King Gustavus Adolphus of Sweden (in fairness he used to say this before every battle, and eventually he ran out of luck).

'Now why did I do that?'
Bonkers baronet Sir William Erskine as he jumped out of a Lisbon hotel window.

We'll close with some spookily prophetic last words from the most famous soothsayer of all, Nostradamus, whose last words were supposedly, 'Tomorrow I shall no longer be here.'

Mind you, I reckon he probably said that every night to be on the safe side...

First published in the United Kingdom in 2016 by
Portico
1 Gower Street
London
WC1E 6HD

An imprint of Pavilion Books Company Ltd

Copyright © Pavilion Books Company Ltd 2016

All rights reserved. No part of this publication may be
copied, displayed, extracted, reproduced, utilised, stored in a
retrieval system or transmitted in any form or by any means,
electronic, mechanical or otherwise including but not limited to
photocopying, recording, or scanning without the prior written
permission of the publishers.

ISBN 978-1-91104-200-6

A CIP catalogue record for this book is available
from the British Library.

10 9 8 7 6 5 4 3 2 1

Reproduction by Mission Productions Ltd, Hong Kong
Printed and bound by 1010 Printing International Ltd, China

This book can be ordered direct from the publisher at
www.pavilionbooks.com

Stupid Last Words

Just as the commentator's curse never fails ('Alistair Cook is playing beautifully today and looking impregnable... oh, he's bowled him!'), the minute these words left the lips these people were as good as dead.

'I'll show you that it won't shoot.'
Singer Johnny Ace, while playing with a pistol and pointing it at his head.

'They couldn't hit an elephant at this distance.'
Major-General John Sedgewick at the beginning of the Battle of Spotsylvania Courthouse.

'But how the devil do you think this could harm me?'
Philosopher Denis Diderot's words to his wife when she warned him against overeating.

'Don't worry, it's not loaded.'
Musician Terry Kath, pointing a gun at his head (he was wrong!).

'The Lord God is my armour.'
King Gustavus Adolphus of Sweden (in fairness he used to say this before every battle, and eventually he ran out of luck).

'Now why did I do that?'
Bonkers baronet Sir William Erskine as he jumped out of a Lisbon hotel window.

We'll close with some spookily prophetic last words from the most famous soothsayer of all, Nostradamus, whose last words were supposedly, 'Tomorrow I shall no longer be here.'

Mind you, I reckon he probably said that every night to be on the safe side...

First published in the United Kingdom in 2016 by
Portico
1 Gower Street
London
WC1E 6HD

An imprint of Pavilion Books Company Ltd

Copyright © Pavilion Books Company Ltd 2016

All rights reserved. No part of this publication may be
copied, displayed, extracted, reproduced, utilised, stored in a
retrieval system or transmitted in any form or by any means,
electronic, mechanical or otherwise including but not limited to
photocopying, recording, or scanning without the prior written
permission of the publishers.

ISBN 978-1-91104-200-6

A CIP catalogue record for this book is available
from the British Library.

10 9 8 7 6 5 4 3 2 1

Reproduction by Mission Productions Ltd, Hong Kong
Printed and bound by 1010 Printing International Ltd, China

This book can be ordered direct from the publisher at
www.pavilionbooks.com